MARRIED BY CHRISTMAS

MOLLIE MATHEWS

Blue Orchid
PUBLISHING

MARRIED BY CHRISTMAS

Mollie Mathews

OVERVIEW

What if the person who is so, so, so wrong for you is really so, so, so right, but you're too afraid to give love a chance?

Last Christmas, art therapist Issy Riley was jilted by her fiancé. This Christmas she's running away. A week with a client on his private Fijian island promises to save her from cheating men and the London festive season. But when the client turns out to be a gorgeous and magnetic Italian billionaire, he threatens her resolve to never again trust her heart to the wrong man.

Milan fashion house leader and avowed bachelor Massimilliano Balforni has no intention of taking a vacation, despite his sister's insistence that he subject himself to an art therapy retreat following a minor heart attack. With an important collection due, he intends to fire his therapist and work, instead. But the determined and striking Issy gives his heart palpitations of a far more dangerous kind.

The one thing Max and Issy agree on: they are as wrong for each other as wrong gets. He's a workaholic playboy who believes emotion is a weakness. She's a romantic who yearns for a happily ever after.

As the tropical heat soars, they discover that in this battle between work and play, resistance only fuels attraction—and sometimes two wrongs make a very passionate right.

Set in two beautiful paradises—Milano, Italy and the tropical Pacific islands of Fiji.

(First published as The Italian Billionaire's Christmas Bride)

PRAISE FOR MARRIED BY CHRISTMAS

"A good read that takes you away to a tropical island to experience the steamy heat of two people determined to stay single in case they get hurt again. Max, a sexy, jaded Italian multi-billionaire meets up with Issy, a playful children's art therapist who has recently found out her fiancé was having an affair. Although I was initially skeptical as I usually go for historical romances, I'm glad I trusted my friend's recommendation because this book was delightfully compelling. The emotional vulnerabilities and character quirks combined with the sexual tension kept the pages turning. A frisky novel to curl up on the couch with or take away on your next trip."

~ Pauline Roberts

"This was a fun read I really enjoyed. It's perfect for a lazy weekend. This is the first book I have read by this author but it won't be last. I can't wait to be more."

~ Poppy

"Beautifully written. The author's vivid and descriptive writing style pulled me into a world I never wanted to leave. I loved the connection of art between two very different people and the healing it brought them both. A Very beautiful story!"

~ Hugh Harrison

"I joined Max to make the slow journey from betrayed broken-hearted individuals to the trusting and loving couple they become. Molly Mathew's writing transports you to places she is describing where you can kick back and relax for a while as this endearing story unfolds. Her characters soon become visible through her careful picture-building. Readers will like the Kiwi vernacular Issy invoices every now and then, and I think readers will enjoy getting to know the strong characters and the beautiful islands we're visiting. The author also tucks in some great life advice for everyone telling in the telling of this charming story. I hope you enjoy this book, too. I did."

~ Alfie Rues

"I loved, loved, loved this book. An instantly gripping, compelling and fun read. Escapism at its best. I couldn't put the book down and read it in one night. With exotic backdrops like Italy and Fiji and passionate characters, it made the perfect holiday read. Can kindness thaw a cold-heart? That's the question Mollie Mathews poses in her book about second chances and learning to love again.

Issy is a funny, compassionate art therapist who wants to escape Christmas after her jerk of a fiancé cheated on her. Even though she only works with troubled children she agrees to take on a last minute client for her friend and business partner. What she doesn't know is her client is hunky fashion house CEO Massimilliano Balforni. Sparks fly and it's an attraction Max vows to deny. He doesn't want Issy and her colored pencils from bringing the wounds of his childhood to the light.

Mollie Mathews skillfully creates a gripping dynamic between Issy and Max that sensually blends their animosity with undeniable attraction making the tension soar. I definitely recommend this book."

~ Lauri

"What a fantastic romance. They seem to be opposites. But they really share a similar past. She's an art therapist and he's a designing mogul . But a week at a private resort in Fiji exposes their hearts and their live. I loved the story, characters and now I want to go to Fiji."

~ Linda

"Issy and Max could not be further from compatible - or could they? He's a multimillionaire fashion designer and she barely makes ends meet as an art therapist. When they are thrown together for a week all kinds of things happen! Will they ever find out if a tiny spark can happen amid all of the chaos? You will need to read this wonderful story by Mollie Mathews to find out! :)"

~ 5-Star Review

One word frees us
of all the weight
and pain of life:
That word is love
~ Sophocles

1

'*Che cavolo!* No! No! No! This will not do. Only an anorexic model could wear something that resembles a straw,' thundered Massimilliano Balforni, CEO of Emporio Balforni, Milan's most prestigious fashion house. His coal black brows knitted in a fierce line as he looked with disdain at the scatter of sketches the young designer splayed on Max's 15th Century walnut desk.

His protégé began to protest but one piercing look from the maestro forced his lips shut. His body stiffened as if frozen to the floor, reminded that his employer's wrath was more dangerous than black ice

'Alexandria Gorbetz is a real woman, the world's richest woman, and someone like me that demands perfection.'

Max's mouth curved in a controlled smile. Was that fear he detected in the young man's face as Max pierced him with his dark gaze? He had every reason to be afraid. Enemies and friends alike knew Max had destroyed promising careers for lesser transgressions. Infinitesimal precision, extraordinary control, unrivaled beauty—Max suffered nothing less.

Pressing his fingertips to the smooth, cool parchment, he paused momentarily as a childhood memory stirred in his consciousness. He sucked in a breath and swept his hands brusquely across the page. He was no longer the lonely child who furtively sketched movie stars in beautiful clothes and dreamed of a Hollywood life.

What was once an escape was now a thriving commercial enterprise with insatiable demands. Max flourished his gold fountain pen across the page, adding a sweep of curves to the hips and breasts of the bespoke wedding gown his fashion house had been commissioned to design.

Now at the helm of his multi-billion dollar empire, Max was no longer a hands-on designer, but nothing went out the door without his final veto. Some called him a control freak and this he took not as a criticism but as the highest compliment.

He waited to feel the rush of joy he used to feel

when drawing as a child. He stopped to await the all-consuming love that arose from knowing that no one possessed his raw talent and genius. He paused to feel the pride that came years later from knowing he designed dresses perfectly, to satisfy only one client on her most important day. There was nothing.

It shouldn't have surprised him. He had long ago accepted that he was unable to feel the joy that other people did. He'd turned off that part of himself years ago and had vowed never again to succumb to vulnerability. In its place, carefully groomed aloofness and instilling fear in others were traits he prized and relentlessly cultivated.

As his protégé braced for the consequences Max forced his thoughts back to the commission. While he felt nothing in his heart, what he did experience as he looked at the drawing of the wedding dress executed to his design was a coolly detached appreciation that satisfied the perfectionist in him.

The lines and structure now conformed absolutely to his definition of ideal. The controlled steel gray pallet reflected his personality and every detailed aspect had been meticulously executed as he had commanded. No randomness or chaos anywhere.

Having witnessed his parents' brutal marriage

and subsequent divorce, Max had no misguided notions of happily-ever-after, nor any desire to marry.

Perfection in relationships was simply unattainable. But the knowledge that he was at the helm of an empire that created exquisite, extraordinarily elegant gowns admired by the world's most elite, at the same time preserving a historic tradition, filled him with a degree of pride.

But as for the rest of his life—the personal, emotional side—he felt nothing. And that suited him perfectly.

Max's long supple fingers drummed an impatient rhythm on the armrest of his chair. '*Allora*?' Well? People react to fear, not love, he reminded himself as he kept his voice soft, but somehow containing all the might of the towering spires of the Duomo looming beyond his window.

A slither of fear crept into the young designer's hushed apology. 'I should have thought more about the woman beneath the dress.'

'Thinking is not enough,' Max commanded, his voice a dark, stark thing in the quiet of his office. 'You must apply.' Taking the drawings in both hands he tore the pages down the middle. 'Begin again, and this time bring me excellence.'

Ignoring the tiny pin like tremors piercing his chest Max pushed back from the desk and rose to his feet as the young man retrieved the torn fragments and scuttled quickly toward the door. Striding across the room Max willed his racing heart to cede to his control.

2

____

'Calm yourself, please Maxie,' Sophia Balforni said, sweeping into his office she cast the young man a sympathetic look as their paths crossed. 'Have you thought about what I suggested?' she asked, gesturing to the art therapy brochure peeking from beneath a pile of contracts.

'I am surrounded by amateurs and now you want me to play like a child, *mia sorella*. I have never heard something so ridiculous.'

'You're my brother. The best brother in the world, but do you know what's holding you back? You're afraid of losing control. You're afraid that without all of this, she said, sweeping her hand around the room, 'you're worthless.'

'But all of this means nothing if you're dead. And none of this means anything without someone to share your heart and soul. I hope one day you're able to realize that you're wonderful for who you are, not just for what you've accomplished. But most of all I hope you're able to experience the unconditional love and support of someone who loves you for you.'

Max was neither given to excessive emotion nor impetuousness but his mood wrestled with his need for control. He threw open the shuttered windows of his office and inhaled the frigid Milano air with shallow, measured breaths.

He ran his hand over his broad chest, fingering momentarily the fine scar snaking across his heart. His mind had the endurance and stamina of one thousand oxen but two months ago his body had betrayed him.

His gaze swept down the Piazza then flew up the spires of the Duomo, dusted with snow and bejeweled in dazzling pre-Christmas lights as the cacophony of Vespas buzzed like irritated wasps through the open window.

Although he had always hated Christmas, he loved tradition and he loved the supreme elegance that the Milanese never failed to deliver, but it pained him to concede that never had his beloved city been so irritating. In fact, everything, and everyone was irritating. Even his designs bored him. He knew better than most that he must continually innovate or die. Grudgingly he accepted his sister was right. He needed to get away.

'I admit it's a little unconventional,' Sophia said, taking an assortment of pills and vitamins from a gold embossed pillbox and, after pouring a glass of mineral water into a crystal tumbler, she passed the pills and water to Max.

'Unconventional?' Max tossed the pills into his mouth, took a gulp of water and threw back his head, grimacing as they slid down his throat. 'What you are suggesting is childish.' *Childish*, isn't that exactly what his father had thrown in his face when, as a young boy, he'd first shown him his sketches. 'If this got out to my competitors,' he said, forcing his mind from a memory he vowed never to revisit, 'can you imagine what it would do to my reputation?'

'Not nearly as damaging as being paralyzed by a stroke and having to be spoon-fed, Sophia snapped. 'And since when have you cared what others think? Besides, you have an island on the other side of the world.

'One which you've been too busy to visit. Fiji is remote enough for you to step away from the constant flash of cameras and be virtually anonymous,' she said, lowering her voice as Max's new PA catwalked into his office. 'Call yourself Mr. Johnstone, or Mr. Smith, or whatever else you want, to protect your privacy.'

Beneath long-fringed lashes the PA gave Max a sultry look, trailing her gaze over his lean and muscled form, as she placed a collection of fashion magazines and media cuttings in a neat pile precisely as she'd been trained.

'Thank you, that will be all,' Sophia said, dismissing her.

'A nudist camp would be vastly more appealing,' Max's gaze trailed after his PA as she left his office. While he had no time for relationships, that didn't stop him from appreciating beauty. How much easier it would be to lie naked amongst a bevy of loveliness than expose his feelings to the spotlight.

Sophia rolled her eyes. 'I can just imagine what that would do to your blood pressure. Art, unlike making a career of intimately studying the curves of women, my dear brother, is therapeutic.'

'So you want me to go to kiddy school and make a fool of myself.' Irritation coursed through his veins as he ran his fingers around the neck of his shirt and loosened the starched white collar.

'You never had a childhood,' Sophia said, her voice almost a whisper. 'You grew up too fast. We both did. And now you're a thirty-five-year-old man who may not see forty.'

'I know you are trying to help but I told you I can handle it.' And he would. He would never abandon his responsibility. Unlike his father who had tried to combine work with marriage and failed at both, Max had gladly sacrificed his personal life for his career.

Abandoned at birth by his biological parents, raised briefly by strangers, then dumped in a boarding school, he had turned what could have been a weakness into his biggest strength.

Self-reliance.

'All this stress has engulfed you, Max. Only you can't see it. And it scares me. You've become a shell of yourself—more than you were already. A man so cut off from his feelings that you are devoid of emotion. You've become a lighthouse of a man—lonely in a crowd, aloof and detached. Uncaring.'

The words bounced off Max's chest like the final shards of Milan's winter sun reflecting off the panoramic glass windows. It was true. He no longer cared.

'What do you want from me, Sophia?'

She paused, concern pooling in her dark eyes. 'I want what our mother wants. I want you to be happy.'

His lips curved into a tight mocking smile. When had his real mother ever cared about his happiness? He knew what she really wanted. After suddenly reappearing in his life, she wanted a daughter-in-law and she wanted a grandson. Max shook his head and gave a short exacerbated sigh. She wanted the impossible.

He plunged his hand through his hair, raking it back from his brow. He should have had it cut razor short last week. Instead, he'd thrown himself into the rollout of his retail network of 60 Massimilliano Balforni boutiques and jewelery stores throughout China, and the pending development of his luxury hotel in Dubai, with such single-minded, unrelenting focus there had been no time for indulgences.

'I've done my research,' he said, adding his signed consent to the final contracts, 'and from every angle it all seems based on spurious psychology.' His hand closed around the pen as he looked up sharply.

Sophia sucked her breath as though steeling herself to battle with his formidable will. 'Unless you make some changes, and I mean massive changes,' Sophia glanced momentarily in the direction of Cimitero Maggiore, Milan's largest cemetery, then fixed Max with a penetrating gaze, 'you'll end up like our father. *Morte.*'

'That will not happen to me,' he said, balling his fingers into a fist. 'I am nothing like our father.'

'No, you're not. You are loyal, honest and immensely generous to the people you care about— nothing like our father. But you are an unrelenting workaholic like he was. No better than an addict, because despite all your willpower, all your determination, all your talent, all your wealth you can't stop working. My God, you even live above your office.'

'*Mia sorella,* even if I wanted to go finger painting, which I do not, there is no way I can get away. People need me. I cannot just walk away without everything collapsing.'

'Even geniuses need time out to replenish. Super-heroes too,' she laughed. 'You, Clark Kent, need a rest from being Superman, a week out of this world. Not eternity. I will take care of things until you're back.'

The blood vessel in his temple pulsed, whether out of conviction or rebellion he didn't know, but her suggestion was not without merit. His sister had proven herself capable in so many ways since her appointment to Director of Public Relations.

He leaned back in his chair, steepling his fingers against his lips as he savored a compelling idea. What if he could achieve several goals by leaving Italy? While he did not believe in fate, he did believe in destiny. Was it not destiny after all that had led him to this career, launching him from male model to CEO of a multi-billion dollar empire?

Max began to wonder if his recent conversation with some Fijian silk merchants was also pre-destined. Until that meeting he hadn't known there was such a large population of Indians in Fiji, and he'd been intrigued by the innovative textile developments they had shared with him.

And he could maximize efficiencies by going undercover and checking out his hotel chain in the Pacific. Yes, he thought, warming to the idea, perhaps a change of scene, getting away from all things European might just revive his flagging spirits.

His creativity was blocked, young designers were licking at his heels. He needed to continually innovate, but nothing inspired him. The plan was worth considering after all. Nothing else had worked. Plus it would get Sophia off his case. And the art therapy gimmick she was so convinced he needed?

What could any dowdy art therapist do to him that he couldn't control?

3

'First time to Fiji?' the porter asked art therapist Issy Riley as they wove past the rows of poolside loungers. Bronzed men and women wearing barely-there swimsuits tanned their lithe bodies beneath the last rays of the sun.

Issy was by far the most uniquely dressed, she thought euphemistically, gazing beyond the pool to the azure sea, fringed with coconut trees. Some, no doubt, would argue she was, in fact, the worst-dressed person at the resort, but then she'd never cared for fashion.

She pushed up the sleeves of the yellow shaggy pile of her jumper as two women sauntered past, tanned from crown chakra to pink toenails, their double d-cups jiggling like caramel panacottas.

Surrounded by an ocean of virtual nakedness Issy felt prudish dressed head-to-toenails in winter discomfort. Certainly less chic than the five-year-old girl meandering past, resplendent in streaming caftan and matching overly bejeweled sandals, snapping the sunset with her iPhone.

'Yes. First time anywhere overseas, actually,' she ran her fingers over the roll of her turtleneck, wishing she'd thought to wear a tee-shirt so she could peel the jumper off.

As always she'd left things too late. She'd been in a mad panic to get to the plane and hadn't even thought to pack spare clothes to change into once she'd arrived at Nadi airport.

Taking refuge beneath a palm tree Issy momentarily relaxed as a choir of Fijian men and women dressed in flowing white gowns began to sing in the open area just beyond the pool. Their voices soared through the humid air. Then suddenly realizing they were singing Christmas carols tension knotted her shoulders.

Christmas.

When she'd offered to help her business partner Nancy, and take this last minute client, she'd thought she could escape the festive season, dripping with tinsel and baubles, and the promise of happiness.

Her fingers tightened around the note the receptionist had passed her when she'd checked in. At least work meant she wouldn't have to spend the holiday season at her mother's with HIM—the traitorous, lying, three-timing control-freak of a fiancé. Make that ex-fiancé, she corrected. She had dumped him immediately, but that didn't stop her heart from taking a hit.

Issy stared into the distance her attention diverted by a huge Christmas tree blazing with a rainbow of colored lights. She closed her eyes and sighed. Why couldn't she find a promise-keeper?

Married by Christmas? Nope. Once again the bus of happily-ever-after failed to pull up at her stop, but to find out on Facebook that James was cheating on her weeks before their wedding? No one deserved that humiliation.

Even if her mother still thought James was the best thing since sliced toast, at least Issy had the balls to shut down his lies, the courage to confront the truth, the strength to face life on her own again. She swallowed hard as the sharp edge of betrayal ran a ragged line through her chest. She'd had a lucky escape.

The porter smiled stiffly as though sensing her discomfort. 'Holiday?'

Issy looked longingly at people relaxing by the pool, her gaze hovering over a loved-up couple entwined on a sun-lounger. She felt a tug of disappointment. Would she ever trust enough to fall in love again? She crushed the note from her client in her hands, pressing her lips together as she turned away. 'Business.'

All the men in her life, even her father, had let her down terribly. Work was a most welcome distraction. She didn't need a man in her life, she reminded herself. Not anymore.

A riot of shouts from the beach pulled her attention toward a group of men jabbing at something writhing on the sand at the edge of the lagoon. Whether it was an instinctive sense of brutality etched in the men's postures or the impact of the powerful figure brushing past her, she didn't know, but every whisper of her body hair stood erect.

Issy watched mesmerized, adrenaline lapping her body as a 6 foot 3 Adonis with olive toned six-pack abs and a body that could easily grace a billboard strode toward the men on the beach, clad only in tiny trunks.

He looked strangely familiar in an unfamiliar sort of way, like a celebrity in a magazine, the same handsomeness, and aloof assurance, although she knew she'd never met him before. He looked like a movie star, only tougher? Certainly not a man anyone would forget.

His muscles rippled gold fire under the heat of

the fading tropical sun as, with powerful, lithe steps like a panther about to lunge, the titan advanced upon the men on the beach. Fear shadowed their faces as they turned to each other, eyes widening, aware this was no normal man approaching but a warrior, a leader of men, a man not to be defied.

'*Allora*! Stop!' His rich honey-toned voice, edged with a deep sultry Italian accent, sent shivers coursing through her body.

Tearing her eyes away from this perfect specimen of a man Issy perched on her toes, squinting under the bright sun to see what the titan was so vigorously trying to protect.

'Sea snake. Very poisonous,' the porter said.

Danger.

The warning flashed red in her mind and jack-knifed through the air. Was it the snake she was afraid of or the rush of molten emotion the stranger incited?

'Come and see,' the porter beckoned.

She hesitated, torn between fear and fascination. Her pulse hammered, pummelled by the unexpected handsomeness of the man and stricken with curiosity. What sort of person would go to a snake's rescue?

For the first time in forever she felt excited, alive, her body on edge, ablaze. Why, when she was officially off men, and as she walked toward him did every whisper of hair on her body stand alert?

She frowned, trying to remember any man ever having inflamed such a reaction, as his muscular arms took the sticks from the assailants. Arms that could crush an opponent or protect a woman against his powerful lean body.

'We're only trying to protect the resort guests from danger,' the men shouted.

'*Che cavolo*! Can you not see the baby snake?' he jabbed his finger towards the rocks. 'Would you deprive it of its mother?' His eyes were a lethal shade of gunpowder blue, his gaze unyielding, freezing the men in a chilly silence. 'She will not strike unless provoked.'

Issy's breath caught in ragged gasps as she glanced at the tiny snake lingering in the distant shadows. Was this guy for real? Someone like her, who cared nothing for the senseless killing of animals.

'We didn't see it. We didn't think,' they said, stepping back. 'Sorry, Sir.'

Issy smiled, her body flooding with something that felt uncomfortably like admiration. She dragged her eyes from him and focused on the snake lying washed ashore, exposed in its vulnerability.

As dangerous as the snake was alleged to be the

artist in her was captivated by the beauty of its iridescent pearl and obsidian stripes. But she was wary too of its potent power. Was the snake feigning death or was it spellbound, against its will, offering herself to the giant of a man before her?

Issy's heart seemed to freeze then pounded like the sea crashing on the distant reef. She could relate to feeling out of her depth. She stole a glance at the knight without armor standing in far too skimpy trunks as with soft, deft movements that belied his powerful physique, he gently nudged the snake toward the sea.

Issy kept her gaze firmly on the snake as it uncoiled slowly, writhing in the wet sand as Issy drew closer to its rescuer. She stood a body's length away from him, agonizingly aware of the rich luster of his full head of blue-black wavy hair, his impeccably shaven jaw, and the intoxicating aroma of his cologne coiling through the balmy air. Earthy, sensual, exhilarating.

What was up with that, she wondered bamboozled by the commotion clanging through her mind. Her eyes recklessly savored every contoured edge of the Adonis's body as he stood at the water's edge watching the snake slither to freedom. She traced his broad, bronzed, well-oiled chest, before sliding down the tantalizingly playful coils of soft dark hair dividing his sculptured six pack and marching a confident line from his navel, before vanishing below the rim of his tiny 'spray on' trunks.

Suddenly the Adonis turned toward her and she was immediately captured in the web of his intense blue eyes.

Issy looked away quickly. Too quickly.

Sprung!

Her face flamed carmine red as she studied her feet, wishing the escaping waves of rose pink hair that fell over her face as she did so would hide her indefinitely. After a brief moment she glanced up, hoping he had not read her mind when she'd gawked at him. The smirk on his face and the intensity of his gaze left her in no doubt he'd registered her attraction.

'Thank you for saving the snake Mr. Johnstone,' said the porter, offering him a towel as he went to his side.

'Johnstone?' her voice eked out. Her eyes ping-ponged between the stranger and the porter. Thrusting her hand in her pocket, she unfurled the note the receptionist had given her. Issy's stomach dived a nervous somersault that would have done an Olympic swimmer proud as she reread the message, studying the words forged in firm, confident handwriting—no sign of weakness anywhere. "Meet me at the pool. (Signed) Mr. Johnstone."

Oh, God. Mortification coiled through her body. 'You can't be *that* Mr. Johnstone.'

He stared at her as if she was insane.

She bit her lip, holding back any attempt at an explanation for her earlier behavior that she knew would only dig a deeper hole. 'There must be some mistake.'

4

―――――

The Mr. Johnstone she was expecting was a middle-aged, totally non-threatening paunchy Scotsman with middle-aged spread. Not a head turner with a license to thrill. Issy glanced back to the hotel lobby hoping to make a hasty retreat in search of the real Mr. Johnstone. The plain, non-threatening one. The one who didn't make her loins quiver ridiculously and her face blaze with heat.

'This is the lady you wanted,' the porter said, gesturing to her.

He stood motionless, his eyes fixed firmly on her with the languid gaze of a panther.

Issy smiled tightly. As if a man who looked like an underwear model would want someone like her, a woman so organic and nonplussed about what was fashionable and what wasn't.

His eyes narrowed beneath perplexed brows as he surveyed the pink waves of hair rippling over her shoulders. She braced herself for criticism. Okay, maybe she was going overboard with the pink hair and the clashing array of colors, but it was her way of rebelling—of shouting out loud, "I don't care".

If she affirmed it often enough, hopefully the fact she cared too much would be erased from her consciousness. And then, on that miraculous day she'd never feel unworthy again.

'Mr. Johnstone,' he said, stretching out his hand. His voice was pure sex, sending shivers scuttling down her spine. It was more honeyed Italian than Scottish in origin, as his name suggested. 'And you are, Miss—?' the Adonis asked, glancing at her hand.

Suddenly her left ring finger felt bare. It was a strange feeling to be conscious of. Nearly a year had passed since she'd thrown her engagement ring back in James' face after his humiliating betrayal.

Issy thrust her hand into her pocket, swallowing hard, before moving her hand to meet his. 'Issy Riley, from Passion Down Under Tours,' she said, injecting her voice with a tone she hoped sounded sufficiently serious.

Passion Down Under—what had she and Nancy been thinking? The name they'd made up for their business sounded fun on paper, but now she had to say it out loud in front of a virtually naked, excruciatingly sexy man it just sounded *wrong*.

His right eyebrow grew into a slight peak at the center, giving him an expression of mischief, though his firm mouth held no trace of amusement. '*Che cavolo! You* are Passion Down Under?'

Was she just being overly sensitive or did something in his tone make it clear he'd expected someone better? Of course he did. He'd expected Nancy. But he needn't look quite so thrown. Issy pushed her shoulders authoritatively back and consciously injected her voice with a somber tone of propriety.

'As far as the rest of the world is concerned anything below the equator is down under,' Issy said, doing a near impossible job of ignoring her loins flaming pure fire under the heat of his inquisitional gaze.

'And we're passionate about our belief in the power of creativity to transform peoples lives, making them feel refreshed, inspired, courageous and playful.' Her words usually imbued with confident purpose when talking to the parents of the kids she helped at Issy's Centre trailed into a faint whisper, then disappeared on a balmy breeze.

The gentle lapping waves washing ashore did little to restore calm. Something about the way his eyes smoldered told her he didn't look in the least like a man needing more passion or courage. And he'd definitely mistaken what she meant by play. However, the tell-tale signs of stress: dark rings under the eyes, tightness of the jaw, shoulders as rigid as mountains, told her he wasn't a man who knew how to relax without an agenda.

'You are not who I expected,' he studied her with microscopic intensity, his face unreadable as his gaze crawled along her purple and yellow striped footless tights, inched along her canary jumper, then rested for an uneasy moment as he read the word "breathe" tattooed in blue running the length of her forearm. His gaze met hers, taking her in with wide-eyed astonishment as though he thought she was certifiably insane.

'There was an accident,' she said, yanking down her sleeve. 'My business partner, Nancy—' she stammered. 'I thought you'd been informed.'

His frown confirmed the worst.

'An accident?'

'Her father—'

'Family must always come first.' His eyes softened as he stared into the vast sea, as though oblivious to her, before turning and staring at her. '*Allora, so you are her replacement?*' His lips pressed together as though suppressing something unpalatable.

'You seem disappointed,' she said, steeling herself from his reproachful stare.

His penetrating gaze stripped her bare. 'I had expected someone more—conservative. Isn't that what counselors look like?'

'I'm not a counselor, I'm an art therapist.' She slid her hand down her neck, wishing like mad she could strip herself of her suffocatingly hot jersey as she wiped away a stream of sweat.

'I don't like surprises,' he said with sardonic derision.

'Breathe', Issy said under her breath, refusing to quake at his steely tone. Breathe. Don't screw this up. 'Oh, whoops. I'm sorry. I don't know why the message never reached you. But we offer a money back warranty, your satisfaction is guaranteed,' she said, instantly regretting the implied promise. 'What I mean is, you won't be disappointed.' She was babbling, over-talking like she always did when she was nervous.

Something about the way he smirked at her communicated white-hot fire, as though for a brief period he might accept the novelty of being with someone so plainly unsuitable. Or was he playing with her? Well, if he thought they were on a sex tour she would dissuade him from that idea.

'I understand you don't know how to relax,' she said, trying to turn the focus back to why they were both here rather than continue to be unsettled by his come-and-get-me sculpted torso and chiseled biceps.

'I know how to relax, *mia cara*.' His voice was husky, the timbre of a low tenor. A sensual shiver shot through her body. Would that voice never stop affecting her this way? Would she ever be able to find his presence bland?

'I'm sorry, I don't understand, my brief was...' She rummaged through the bag slung over her shoulder, and felt the steady almost appalled air of his disapproving gaze as he looked at the chaotic, disordered state of what she sensed to him was less of a handbag and more of a hand-sack. 'I know I have the email somewhere.'

He stepped toward her, the full impact of his virile masculinity leaving her nearly breathless. 'Sex.'

'Excuse me?' she stammered.

'Sex is my relaxation strategy, *mia cara*.'

He was being deliberately provocative, she was sure of it now, but if he was determined to unnerve her he would find a worthy opponent. 'How charming for you,' she said coolly, flourishing the note. 'You summoned me.'

'Tomorrow we will leave for my private island. My chauffeur will pick us up at 7 sharp to take us to the airport. Please do not be late.'

Something cold slid down the back of Issy's neck. Private island? Nancy hadn't mentioned this. 'I don't like surprises either,' she said, caught between apprehension and curiosity. 'Look, I'm sure you're legit and everything, but I really don't feel comfortable taking off to goodness knows where with a man I've only just met. What's wrong with sticking to the itinerary? A week here, at this very nice,'and very public,' resort?'

'I prefer the comfort of home,' he said, barely answering her question. 'It was never my intention to stay on the mainland longer than I needed. Oh, and be sure to bring some clothes better suited for the climate,' he said, as he turned from her.

Fine hairs bristled on her neck. Okay, so she was sweltering hot, but that wasn't the point. Not only was he changing the whole agenda, but now he had the arrogance to tell her how to dress.

The two slim-legged blondes in barely-there bikinis she'd seen earlier sauntered past, flicking their hair coyly as they smiled in Max's direction. Whatever tenuous hold Issy had had on him quickly disappeared as his gaze combed their bodies with primal appreciation. Irrational jealousy sloshed through her body, mixing with painful memories of the fickleness of men.

'Enjoy your evening, Mr. Johnstone.' Excusing herself, she choked back a defiant retort, stealing a backward glance as she strode away.

What do I care, she reminded herself? He was a client, not her lover. She should be focusing on the task ahead, figuring out how she was going to get through the next week rather than allowing herself to become stupidly distracted by a man. A man completely off limits. A man totally out of her league.

5

Casting the bimbos prancing before him a dismissive glare Massimilliano turned his attention back to the irritatingly intoxicating, beguiling woman who had in one sweeping touch managed to pierce every impenetrable fortress he'd erected.

She had walked away from him, her manner clearly dismissive. He was not accustomed to being dismissed, especially by someone technically in his employ. Women usually followed him around and worshipped his every movement. Somehow he didn't imagine Issy Riley doing anything of the sort.

He ran his hand over his thumping chest. Two months ago he'd suffered a minor heart attack and now this proud woman was giving him palpitations. It was not the speed of his attraction that frightened him most, although this was indeed worrying, what frightened him most was the irrationality of her appeal.

Massimilliano was not an impulsive man, nor a man ruled by his emotions and certainly not one to take a second look at a woman so aesthetically un-coordinated. Issy Riley was so unlike any of the women he normally dated. How long had it been since one had quickened his pulse-rate?

He'd known super-models, divas and heiresses and not one was as plain nor as pretty, in an odd sort of chaotic way, as Issy Riley. With her masses of rosé tousled, just-got-out-of-bed hair tumbling in every direction she was not at all what he had expected. But then there was something refreshingly invigorating about her. Something dangerous that made Massimilliano wonder what it would be like to touch her.

Yes, he thought with surprising relief, she was definitely more bohemian artist than high-class model with flighty temperaments, and hearts as hardened and frozen as his. Issy Riley oozed passion and authenticity. She was an unusual woman, perhaps a sapphire in the raw. Instinct told him she was one of those rare people who just aren't aware of her potent sensuality and the power she yielded.

And that made her hazardous.

Massimilliano's head began to spin. What was

he thinking? He knew nothing of her. No doubt she would be like every other woman he had ever met, needy, demanding attention and continuously distracting him from his work. Or tortured and conniving, in search of a fortune or wanting to party, party, party.

Before he knew it he'd have a ball and chain around his ankle being dragged down the aisle of the Cathedral Duomo, preventing him from getting to the glory that he knew was within him, the one that would immortalize him as King.

No. He didn't do the C word. Commitment. Not since coming dangerously close with Lucrezia. She had been all of those women, coiled into one poisonous package.

Work, in capitals, bolded and italicized with an exclamation mark, was his savior, the only thing he would ever commit to. 'WORK! WORK! WORK!' he affirmed, forcing his mind from Issy to the task at hand, as the Indian merchants he'd met with earlier advanced toward him and handed him more fabric samples.

His work was all consuming, the only area of his life he could be certain of maintaining full control. Max's fingers slid along the soft, sinuous fibers of the silk, and his traitorous mind wondered with one heart-stopping moment whether Issy Riley's flawless skin would respond as the silk did, writhing and twisting in response to his touch.

Something about that woman and the effortless way she'd attracted his interest threatened his fastidiously erected barricade. Suddenly this whole artist's therapy gobbledygook retreat his sister had talked him into looked like a perilous idea.

She, unlike any woman before her, was more dangerously unpredictable than the serpent he had rescued from the engulfing sea. Her green, almost feline eyes, deep with insight seemed to see right into his soul exposing a vulnerability he'd learned to keep hidden.

He could not fire her, but he would ensure he kept her at a distance.

6

'Oh my God, Nancy!!! I can't believe it! I mean...wow! You never told me he'd be so good looking. I made a right fool of myself.' Careful not to knock over the glass she was soaking her watercolor brushes in Issy leaned closer to her iPad.

'Kids I can help, but him? How am I supposed to concentrate? Did you set me up?' Issy said, a frown furrowing her brow as she stared at the image of her business partner on Skype.

'I swear,' Nancy said, crossing her heart. 'The woman who made the booking was very secretive. She didn't tell me her brother was going to be a hunk.' Nancy said, picking up her coffee cup and slurping noisily.

'Try drop dead sexy! Toweringly tall, heart

wrenchingly   handsome.   Particularly   perfect.'
Achingly dangerous. Issy pushed her paints to one
side, glanced out of the hotel room and gazed at the
ocean. It was hard to believe that something which
looked like a haven of calm had the potential to
swell without warning, flooding and causing devas-
tation in its wake.

'She told you none of that?' Equal measures of
terror and exhilaration surged through Issy's chest
as she thought of her client standing at the water's
edge, the sea snake at his feet, as he went to its
rescue.

'I thought you were off men?'

'I am, but my traitorous body is annoyingly impervious. It's like looking at the sun. You know you
shouldn't but it's so dazzlingly hypnotic.'

'Bonus!'

'No, Nancy, it's not a bonus.' Issy's already agi-
tated heartbeat quickened. 'This adds a whole different level of complexity. For one, I'm out of my
depth. Two, he made it quite clear that he regards
sex, not delving into his psyche, as the ultimate
form of relaxation.'

She felt her heart lurch and told herself it was
anxiety, certainly not the thought of tangling in the
sheets with the owner of such an amazing
physique.

'And three,' she said, noticing with alarm the

high trill of her voice. 'I just can't see him taking art therapy seriously.'

'It's not meant to be serious.'

'I know. At heart everybody's a child, and having fun via art therapy is the perfect way to restore the balance. I know all of this. I wrote the manifesto for our business remember.'

'Of course we'll succeed. You're brilliant, Issy Riley,' Nancy said, stepping from the screen and returning with a fist-full of papers. 'Besides, the brief was pretty fluid,'

'Define fluid,' Issy said, her gaze drifting to the splash of carmine red watercolor seeping across her painting, igniting a memory of the fire in Mr. Johnstone's eyes when he'd told her that sex was his favorite form of relaxation.

Issy's heart began to pulse against her chest as a dangerous blaze ignited inside her. Sitting upright in her chair and giving Nancy her full attention she forced her mind back to the business at hand.

'His sister contacted me,' Nancy said, flourishing a piece of paper in front of the screen. 'She said she liked the sound of our art therapy program and thought it would be perfect for her brother,' she said, scanning the document. 'Something about capturing the childhood he never had.' Lifting her head to the screen Nancy looked at Issy. 'Are you Okay? You look flushed?'

'Yip,' Issy said, sucking in her breath. 'It's just super humid over here.'

Nancy frowned, narrowing her gaze dubiously. 'Okay. All I was told was he needed to de-stress, to stop being so serious, and learn to have some fun. I figured, how hard can it be? And let's face it. You could do with having some fun too. You haven't been yourself. Not since—'

'Not since someone videoed my fiancé screwing his PA at the Christmas party last year and up-loaded the gross debacle to YouTube. You can say it. I'm beyond caring.' Issy manufactured a well-prac-ticed I-don't-care smile, a smile which she hoped hid her growing belief that she would never find a man who wouldn't let her down.

Something was obviously wrong with her, per-haps some past-life karmic debt Why else was she always attracting men who cheated on her? Well, she didn't need to find out because she wouldn't bother trying again. She was happy on her own.

No drama's, no second guessing, no trying to be someone that somebody wanted. Nope, she was free. Wasn't that what she always wanted?

Issy swallowed hard, ignoring the rising metallic taste that swum in her mouth when she didn't buy a word of what she'd just told herself.

'Forgetting what that jerk did to you by burying your heart in work this Christmas is perfect timing.

And there's nothing in the rule book that says you can't enjoy yourself. Hanging out in paradise with a handsome stallion sounds like just the rescue remedy you need.'

Issy frowned. 'I don't need rescuing, Nancy.'

'You do, Issy. Remember our promise? Remember how we both said no matter how many men broke our hearts that we'd never give up on love.'

'I haven't given up on love.'

'I know but you're paying it lip service. You say you're open to taking another chance. You say you still believe in happily ever after. Marriage. Kids. A white picket fence.'

'I'd like a castle,' Issy added.

'Okay, a castle—and a prince.' You're saying all the right things, but you're not taking any action. You haven't been on a date in how long? You have to do something. Go out. Kiss a toad. Kiss a frog. Kiss anyone.'

'Settle.'

'I'm joking.'

'You sound like my mother. I'm just not ready.'

'Who's ever ready? You'll be ready when you stop hiding and get out and try.' Nancy said.

'Right now I'd just like to be able to pay the bills.'

'Yip, and you're the one always banging on about

the Universe and manifesting miracles. We haven't worked with adults before and then out of the blue here come Mr. Rich, an expressway to the high-end corporate market. Who knows where this could lead!'

Issy's gaze shot to the time at the top of the screen. 'Oh, my God! Is that the time? Nancy, I've gotta go!'

Issy shut down her iPad and rose from the desk, nearly knocking the cup of water she'd been dipping her brushes into. She glanced at the time again. 'Damn! Damn!Damn!' Yanking the painting smock over her head she threw it into a plastic bag, zipped it shut and wedged it into her already billowing suitcase.

Don't be late, Mr. Johnstone had commanded, as though affirming the inevitable. So maybe it was true—she was always getting lost in time. Especially when doing what she loved, losing herself in the sensual fluid beauty of watercolor.

While she was a failure at relationships, give her some paints and a canvas and she could rustle up something close to success. She smiled briefly as she studied the abstract wash of fiery reds and tangerine and melon hues, streaked with gold, capturing the morning sunrise.

Art was less fickle, more loyal, less unpredictable than any man, she mused rolling up her brushes and placing them with the watercolor in a satchel. While her idea of heaven right now was time alone with her box of paints it was an indulgence she could not afford. Mr. Johnstone didn't strike her as a man who'd wait for anyone.

7

Thrusting her feet into a turquoise floor length kaftan dress printed with a riot of abstract hummingbirds she bunched her hair into a wild knot, slapped on some tinted lip balm, and with her heart hammering wildly she grabbed her suitcases.

Pulling the handles she dragged them out of her hotel room and walked briskly to the end of the landing. 'Why did I pack so much?' she cursed, almost tripping on the hem of her dress as she heaved her suitcases down two flights of stairs.

Issy paused for a heartbeat on the landing and took a hurried look at the hotel clock. It was only 7:00 am. 6:51 to be precise but the morning air hissed with heat. She intensified her pace and hurried onto the hibiscus-lined walkway leading to the hotel lobby. The blazing bush of flowers passed in a blur of fiery red as she rattled over the marble tiles, clutching the billowing fabric of her dress knotting around her ankles.

But the wilful suitcase wheels had minds of their own, pirouetting in opposing directions as she tried to run. She yanked again and then released the handles, sighing with exasperation. The bags crashed to the ground with a thunderous thud. The zip sent out a splintering groan, then burst spewing the contents of her case meters from the foyer.

'Oh, damn!' Her hands flew to her mouth as she dropped on her knees and hurried to retrieve her clothes strewn in a tangled heap in the garden.

'Can I help?' The rich lyrical accent slid over her like red silk.

Issy's face flamed. Yip, this was so her unlucky day. She fixed her eyes on his sleek loafers as an unmistakable powerful frame cast a shadow over her.

'Nope, it's all good,' she muttered, her voice dry.

'Yours I believe?' he said, draping her wayward G-string before her eyes.

She looked up slowly, mortification weaving through every fiber of her body. Her traitorous eyes inched the length of his powerfully built athletic legs, trailed the fitting cut of his extraordinarily well-tailored casual trousers, crawled the length of his muscular thighs, beckoning her eyes beyond.

Beyond anything she was ever going to look at, or feel, or touch.

Avoiding his gaze, she reached out to extract her knickers suspended from his wide, tapered fingers. Her hands brushed against his warm skin, causing every hair on her body to flame with pulsing heat. 'Thanks,' she stammered, her mouth dry as Fijian sand.

'I thought we were meeting in the lobby,' she said, staring up into his gorgeous face rampant with masculine beauty, framed magnetically by thick waves of dark hair. 'I'm not late am I?'

His fingers circled the heavy silver links of his Omega watch, then clamped the black face, his dark brows furrowing as he checked the time across four continents 'Not yet,' he said, pinning her with his searing gaze.

So he wasn't going to do a runner and leave without her, Issy though with a mix of disappointment and relief.

'Your punctuality is appreciated. As is your underwear.' Jaw-droppingly gorgeous dimples framed his lips as they curved into a brief smile, and the humor in his tone made her stomach somersault, demolishing what few defenses she had in an instant. She plastered a super-composed smile on her face, ignoring the butterflies in her gut and piled the last of her clothes into her suitcase, then sat on it, forcing the zipper shut.

As she went to stand he held out his hand. 'Allow me to help, *mia cara*'

Issy hesitated. She'd vowed never to accept help from any man again, no matter how innocuous. 'It's all good,' she said. As she struggled to rise her sandals snagged on the hem of her dress.

'I insist, *principessa.*'

Reluctantly she took his palm in hers and allowed him to sweep her to her feet. Her hand pulsed with electricity. His breath felt warm against her face, his cologne spicy and sultry as she drew beside him. She sensed his body tense as though as unsettled as she was by the chemistry that throbbed between them.

His brows knotted into a troubled line as he took a step back. 'I see you dressed for the climate.' His lush lips pressed together in a hard and grim line.

She noticed his eyes wince as he studied the dizzying array of colors and patterns splashed over her dress. 'You look like you've just eaten a lemon,' she bit.

'On the contrary. It's actually disarmingly charming.' He reached out to touch her dress, trailing his fingertips along the neckline, then pressing slightly on her shoulder as though she was a mannequin. To her chagrin rather than protest her body reveled in his touch, pirouetting with the grace of a ballerina.

His eyes were a pool of molten silver as her gaze again met his. 'Crazy,' he said darkly. His hot gaze alighted on Issy, making her skin tingle and her body feel way too hot. 'Madness.' He pulled his hand away, as though the sensual attraction that burned through her body burned through his too.

She'd be mad to entertain such dangerous thoughts. 'I love color,' she said, deliberately misunderstanding him. 'And if it's crazy, then good. When I wear this dress, it's a living, breathing affirmation. A giant, floor length reminder that life is to be lived with color and joy and spontaneity.

'As the artist, Paul Klee says, one eye sees and the other feels. I'm done with feeling blah. I'm over feeling invisible. I'm spent with feeling that I have to fit everyone else's expectations about how I should act and think and feel. 'I've been there, done that, wore the monotone tee-shirt and suffocated,' she bit, gesturing to his immaculately tailored black attire.

'I want to be crazy, I want to be wild, I want to breathe,' she said, not caring that she was blabbering. She tilted her chin and fixed him with a determined stare. 'I'm a recovering conformist.'

'I can see that,' he said arching an eyebrow. 'You've certainly gone to a great deal of effort to show your contempt for fashion. But I've always admired people who have a sense of themselves,' his eyes drifted over her pink hair while searching for words. 'To express your feelings regardless of other's opinions is admirable.'

'Admirable?' Issy studied him skeptically. Was he complimenting her? She didn't dress like this to get compliments. She dressed like this to keep men away.

'What about you? 'Why would you want to look like you're always going to a funeral?' she challenged. 'Black does nothing for you,' she lied, as they walked through the foyer to the waiting limousine.

'You speak your mind.' Max signaled to the waiting staff member to pick up their luggage.

'Didn't you last night, when you told me what to wear? I think what you wear should be fun,' she said, as they passed the gift shop.

'Fun?' he said, his tone incredulous.

'Honestly, how do you feel dressed neck to toe in black?'

'I like the lines, the structure, the simplicity. Colour is distracting. I prefer tonal subtlety. Graphite grays and obsidian blacks, they are my preferred palette.'

Issy stepped toward the tourist shop in the lobby, bulging with a kaleidoscopic montage of Fijian shirts.

'That wasn't what I asked. I asked, how does black make you feel?'

Max remained outside the store, stoic and silent.

'When did you last let out your inner child?' Issy asked gently, sensing his heart was so frozen, his emotions so foreign to him he couldn't even name them.

His lips pressed into a firm, unyielding line.

Just as she thought. Fun had been off his agenda, just as it had been from hers for far too long. She had no idea what had caused him to be so resolutely serious, but she was up for the challenge. She sensed by helping him she would help herself. And she knew just the place to start. 'Pick one,' she said, as she headed toward a rack of brightly colored shirts.

'We'll be late.'

'Not if you don't hold us up,' she challenged.

His dark gaze was intent on hers as he strode toward her, his posture stiff and uncompromising.

'I'm sure your clothes are expensive,' she said, as she rifled through the racks, 'but something with more vibrancy wouldn't go amiss. Something like this.' Issy pulled out a shirt ripe with pineapples and swaying palm trees.

No matter how gaudy the shirt was, she thought holding the shirt up to him, she was sure his muscular physique would pop. The challenge could be finding something to accommodate his extra wide shoulders.

She felt him tense and laughed, something she suddenly realized she hadn't done in months. It was fun playing dress-ups with a man so firmly against anything she may introduce, she thought enjoying the look of mortification on his face.

As she paraded a mayhem of colored shirts before him the challenge it posed to transform this resolutely determined man excited her unexpectedly.

'Miss Riley,' he growled, tapping his watch.

'This is Fiji, for goodness sake. I'm not leaving until you agree to try something different. Something relaxed.'

His lips pressed into a grim line, as she pressed another shirt against his chest.

'You're right. The lime is too cool for the warm tones of your face. It makes you look sallow,'she said, screwing up her face. On the other hand sallow is good, she thought.

If she encouraged him to buy a shirt that achieved the impossible, a shirt that made him look less ravishing, it would be easier not to be thrown by his dark, brooding beauty.

It was impossible not to be agonisingly aware of every plane of his perfect, athletic physique, especially his powerful chest, steely and hard, as she pressed the shirts against him. Every ounce of his body screamed pure fire. Issy tried to focus her attention on finding the happiest, most gaudy shirt she could find.

'Bingo, perfect!' She said, producing a vibrant blue shirt. 'The color brings out the sapphire highlights in your eyes perfectly,' she said seeing her own reflection in his molten gaze.

Dark brows folded in a frown as he studied the lagoon blue background, highlighted with banana yellow surrounded by a scattering of red hibiscus flowers.

'You look like Superman, only without the cape,' she giggled.

'Fine, whatever makes you happy, Miss Riley. I'll take it. But don't expect me to wear it anytime soon,' he scowled, crossing his arms defiantly over his powerful chest.

Issy smiled. We'll see about that.

8

'Welcome to the happiest place on earth.' Issy chewed her lip as she glanced up at the billboard at Nadi airport as they prepared to board Max's private jet.

A picture of a loved-up couple in swimsuits, their damp bodies pressed together as they perched on the bow of a super-yacht, towered over her. On her left two naked bodies entwined in rope on a palm tree-lined beach simmered from a giant billboard. Layers of beautiful monochromatic clothes, the color of sand, lay strewn about them.

Issy tore her gaze away from the exotic scene, and focused on the logo powerfully positioned at their feet. Balforni, she recited staring into the eyes of the formidable black eagle emblazoned above the gold logo. Obviously Mr Johnstone only bothered with high-end labels, she noted looking down at her own tired collection of uncoordinated bags.

Balforni. Balforni. Balforni. She chanted silently, trying to summon the eagle's strength to block her mother's taunts, as her mother's shrill voice rang through her ears. "If you're not careful Isabel, you'll end a spinster." Her mother's relentless criticism and the lack of affection she had shown Issy throughout her childhood only reaffirmed Issy's belief that perhaps she was unlovable, destined to always be alone.

She glanced at Mr Johnstone as he strode down the walkway, his phone pressed to his ear, a torrent of Italian bouncing off the walls as he spoke. Right now she may as well be alone, she thought, turning away from the plethora of happy couple billboards. Her client didn't look the least bit interested in spending time with her, let alone relaxing.

In fact, just the opposite.

She studied him as he paused at a doorway leading onto the tarmac, a tight woosh of air escaping his chest, as his chauffeur handed him a slim leather satchel, and placed a collection of black embossed leather luggage on the ground. Seeing all his luxurious carry-on next to her battered suitcases made the disparity between their social standing widen before her eyes.

'Is that a laptop?' Issy asked, pointing to the slim-line leather case in his hands. 'I thought the whole point of being here was to switch off from work.' She hoped her tone sounded professionally concerned rather than nagging school mum.

She cared. Of course she cared. And it wasn't just about the fee payable when she had succeeded in helping him unwind, she reminded herself as he turned to her, his powerful neck tensing as though he carried the weight of the world.

'I didn't get the memo,' he replied, mildly enough, yet she could hear the heft of his ruthlessness beneath it, and the deadly thrust of his dismissal. Dark rings cast a shadow beneath his eyes as he watched the uniformed crew walking toward them across the tarmac.

Stress killed regardless of wealth. She knew this better than anyone. Raging blood pressure had left her father, once a proud and strong man, had been paralyzed by a stroke. Mercifully, for him, but devastatingly for her, a heart attack had taken him quickly. No matter how resistant her client was she would get satisfaction from helping him switch off.

No one was dying on her watch.

'Mr. Balforni, your jet is ready to depart,' one of the men said, opening the security doors and signaling to the others to take his luggage.

Issy turned her head sharply.

'*Balforni?*' Her stomach rose in her throat. 'You're

who?' she stammered, but the roar of the engines droned out her questions. Hitching up the hem of her dress she scuttled to keep up with her client as he strode across the tarmac.

He waited at the base of the private jet, ignoring her questioning eyes, as she approached. He placed a proprietary hand on the small of her back. His palm, warm and soft connected with her bare skin, sending a frisson of heat scuttling up her spine as he guided her up the aircraft stairs.

'Balforni, as in Emporio Balforni? she stammered, awareness dawning on her as she looked around the interior. Had she not been so thrown she might have savored the supreme elegance of the minimalist interior, but she was too stunned.

Her eyes locked on the fine leather trim of the aircraft dotted with the eagle's crest Balforni logo she'd seen on the billboards, and in magazines too expensive to buy.

It made sense now, she thought looking at his powerful physique, his dark wave of hair, his chiselled jaw, the incredibly handsome face. He looked familiar because he *was* familiar. But what she didn't understand was how the CEO of Italy's most famous fashion house was now her client.

'You said your name was Johnstone. Why didn't you tell me who you really were?' she challenged, perching on the edge of a sumptuous black leather seat.

Massimilliano squeezed his powerful frame into the chair opposite her, his majestically long athletic legs almost touching hers, causing the fine downy hairs on her legs to stand erect.

'When you live under the constant spotlight as I do, you prize moments of anonymity.' His tone hinted at an underlying discontent Issy had detected before.

'I can't believe you let me lecture you on fashion.' She shook her head, clasping her hair in her hands, 'You must think I'm a complete idiot.'

'On the contrary,' he said, thumbing through an Italian Vogue placed on the table before him. 'It was refreshing.' He looked up briefly, his blue eyes glittering.

Humiliating, yes, refreshing, no, Issy thought trying not to feel overwhelmed by the presence of one the fashion's most acclaimed geniuses and one of the world's most formidable businessmen.

God help me, she said under her breath as once again he turned his attention to his work systematically thumbing through the magazine. His eyes barely blinked as he studied the world's most glamorous women flawlessly adorned with the world's latest fashion trends.

How was she going to succeed in getting the

grand maestro of fashion to switch off when he had so much beauty to distract him? What did she really have to offer, she thought, feeling more and more inadequate as she compared herself to the beautiful women rising from glossy pages.

Rich, virile, incredibly good-looking men like Massimilliano Balforni dated top models, bedded the ones who excited him sexually, and one day would marry the most beautiful of them. Men like him never chose women like her. But it was a moot concern. He was her client. She *so* wasn't going there. Besides she wasn't even remotely tempted. She ignored the tension tightening her gut, calling her a liar.

Oh, just to have a smidgen of his talent, she thought forcing her mind from her illicit thoughts. He withdrew a sketch pad and gold fountain pen from his satchel, and flourished the nib across the page, executing sketches with the ease of a person writing a shopping list.

She studied the firm, confident lines—no sign of weakness anywhere. She was no graphologist but it was clear her client was not a man used to taking orders, nor a man used to ceding control.

And while she sensed there was a lack of joy and spontaneity there was something magnetically at-tractive about the way sensuality blended with pre-cision, she thought briefly before reality hit reminding her she would do well to maintain a professional detached interest. He loved his work. No wonder he was an obsessive workaholic. Everything about his work oozed profit.

Profit.

Something she had never given much attention. If she had she wouldn't always be living from pay cheque to pay cheque. Just one of his sketches would command a significant fee. Of course, she would never do something so lacking in integrity.

Nor would she betray his trust, no matter how much she needed the money, she thought glancing out at the horizon as she recalled a recent story in the press of the leaked concepts of a famous British designer.

'Are you addicted to work?' she said, as he took a call, fighting the urge to take the magazines and throw them out the window as the plane began to climb. How on earth was she ever going to manage to get him to relax if he was addicted to his craft?

'*Scuse?*' Emotionless dark eyes looked at her beneath acerbic brows.

'You're supposed to be on a retreat,' she said, annoyed with herself for sounding like a nagging wife.

'*Mia tentatrice,* the mind of a creative entrepreneur never switches off, Ms. Riley—no matter what the temptation. My work is all consuming,' he said, in a tone morphing between condescension and flirtation.

She pointed out the window as they flew over sapphire seas dotted with turquoise reefs ringed with baby blue coral. 'Look around you at all this inspiration,' she said, ignoring her throbbing pulse.

He sighed impatiently. 'I don't need distractions. I gain my inspiration from my inner world,' he said in an indulgent tone.

No wonder your designs lack color, she thought to herself.

He turned away, his leg brushing hers, sending the uncomfortably familiar friction of desire threading across her loins.

He glanced down at his sketches. His fingers clenched the edges of the page, then crushed the drawings, reducing them to hardened balls.

'Why did you destroy them?' she said, looking at the crumpled Balforni originals.

'They lacked perfection,' he growled, his mood blacker than his fierce eyes.

Issy pressed her lips together, holding back the urge to cry out, "They were perfectly, imperfect. I could have sold them for a squillion." While she sensed that like many geniuses he was obsessive in his quest for perfection, what she didn't understand yet was what drove him to strive for the seemingly impossible. What was wrong with good enough?

She sensed he could turn into the consummate chameleon, turning on an open charm at the flash of a camera for his clients, playing the role of a gregarious, fun-loving extrovert as though it were his true nature. But, if her instinct was correct the world would rarely see the real man. Was he too controlled, too private, too damaged, she wondered, to allow that.

She would have to take it slowly if she was to succeed in helping him make the changes he needed, but obviously denied. As she looked at his drawn face, his wide shoulders hard as granite, she realized that they carried a great burden.

While he was polite and friendly enough she sensed that somewhere behind his eyes was a carefully cordoned off area to which few people—especially not a therapist—were ever admitted. She would need to probe deeper, discovering his desires as well as his fears.

'Why did you decide to found a fashion empire?' She asked, infusing her voice with a soft child-like curiosity she hoped he wouldn't find threatening.

Silence hovered between them thickening the air. The whole process of having to talk about himself was clearly one he recoiled from. He shrugged and nudged the conversation on. 'Why did you become an art therapist?'

9

'I trained as a clinical psychologist, but art therapy is a much better fit. So, yes, I'm a psychologist, but sometimes there isn't a group of people I loathe more than those in my profession. I don't believe that people have to be psycho-analyzed, medicated up to their right eyeball because no one can be open-minded enough to try less conventional and more holistic ways to unlock the trauma that lies buried in the subconscious.'

Her eyes glistened, the passion she felt for her work, her vocation, her calling, obvious in the way that she spoke.

'I know what it's like to spend your life trying to live up to the weight of other peoples expectations, only to fail miserably.'

Something about her words, quietly spoken

now, dragged Max's attention from a haze of memory. Perhaps they weren't too dissimilar.

'Do you know who is the worst?' Issy continued, her breathing fast.

Max looked up from his pile of sketches, his fingers tightening around his pen and shook his head.

'Psychologist JB Watson. Gosh, now there's a man with issues. It's been over 70 years since he dispensed his twisted child-rearing advice and people still follow that crap,' she said, her cheeks flushing.

'Let your behavior always be kindly firm,' she said, deepening her tone and imbuing her voice with masculine severity. 'Never hug and kiss them. Never let them sit on your lap. If you must kiss them do it once on the forehead when they say goodnight.

'Shake hands with them in the morning. Give them a pat on the head if they have made an extraordinarily good job of a difficult task.' She shook her head, sending a cascade of pink waves tumbling across her shoulders.

'The man was a complete jerk and worse, he was wrong. Deprive people of social touch, especially newborns and what do you get?'

Max remained mutely silent, crossing his arms over his chest as he leaned on an angle toward the exit aisle. Emotional deprivation was something he was painfully acquainted with. He was pretty sure Issy would agree that being the child nobody wanted, fostered then abandoned by his new parents to grow up in an English boarding school wouldn't rate highly on the social touch index.

Nor would being called gay when his drawings of flowing ball dresses and diamond-studded gowns were discovered. Being attacked in the dorms at boarding school on an almost daily basis, and beaten by his father, was as social as things got.

What do you get? He could answer her question with one phrase.

Self-reliance.

He knew as he sensed she did, that only the extraordinary few rose above their traumatic childhoods.

'What you get is kids that grow into adults unable to love—themselves nor anyone else.' Issy said, answering her own question. 'My kids aren't stuck in the understaffed Romanian orphanages in the '80s and '90s, but the impact is the same—they've been starved of love and affection.'

Max sat back in his chair, as he regarded the intelligent, passionate woman sitting before him. Instead of seeing her as a self-righteous, know-it-all, psychologist, he now saw a compassionate woman, a nurturer, a woman dedicated to improving the lives of those most vulnerable. A woman who seemed to be too intimately aware of a world he was once personally acquainted with and had no wish to revisit. But she was as fascinating as she was dangerous.

'Abandoning a career as a clinical psychologist to become an art therapist must have taken courage and incredible tenacity' he said, maintaining an even tone, as he succumbed to his curiosity. He avoided her gaze and fixed his attention on the sketch in front of him.

'It wasn't easy,' she said, studying her lap briefly as though being complimented was rare and a little unsettling. 'My parents thought I was mad turning my back on a "reputable profession," she said, fluttering her fingers in the air. 'But I can't do something I don't believe in.'

He looked into her open, kind face. 'And what is it you believe?'

'Art therapy touches the spirit, soothes the trauma of the past, and empowers hope and confidence in the future. That's why I like working with children. Most of the issues adults face today have their roots in childhood. I want to be the ambulance at the top of the cliff. I want to help before kids become adults saddled with baggage and mistaken beliefs.'

Issy shook her head as the steward approached offering her a crystal flute bubbling with champagne. 'No, thank you. I don't drink,' she said opting instead for a glass of sparkling water.

Max regarded her with growing interest. 'So you mainly work with young people?' He should have felt extreme annoyance to learn that she lacked expertise and competence working with people his own age. Instead, he found his growing admiration for her disconcerting. How much easier it would be to maintain an aloof, arrogant disregard for a know-it-all therapist than for someone he found utterly captivating, a woman in control of her mind, not afraid to swim upstream and stand up for her beliefs.

'Yes, it's the reason I opened my center, Issy's Kids.' Issy chewed her lip and glanced out at the ribbon of vapour-thin clouds streaming past the window as the jet leveled out.

Something was troubling her and Max suddenly felt very protective, which was strange and unsettling.

'The children I work with respond well to its non-invasive nature,' she said, turning those far too knowing eyes toward him. 'Psychotherapy is so analytical, completely ignoring the right hemisphere of the brain, whereas art therapy goes straight to the heart,' she said, pressing her palm to her chest to emphasize the point.

Max's mouth tightened. *Now he was in trouble.*

Issy smiled at him, apparently unaware that just being near to her was a threat to his physical space, let alone what she was determined to do with him professionally. After a lifetime avoiding anyone breaking through the fortified walls he'd erected around his heart it was becoming clearer to him that he'd underestimated her. They may be forced to spend time together, but being alone on his island with her would be a massive mistake.

'Of course, in case you're wondering,' she said, her green eyes fixed on him. 'I'm not naive enough to think that art therapy can solve all their problems but it does help uncover the issues that keep them stuck.'

Pressing firmly on the page he drew a strong, black line. 'Do you have children?' He asked, steering the conversation firmly to safety.

She took a shaky breath and tucked that delicious strawberry hair behind her ears. 'I always wanted kids, but only if I could offer them some stability. I know it seems old fashioned, but I don't want to raise a child on my own. If I had children, I would want them to have two parents. Loving parents,' she added, quickly.

'Not parents like mine. Waring, self-focused parents.' She turned away from him, clenching the armrest with trembling fingers as she gazed out the window. 'I'd love to have my own children but things haven't quite worked out that way,' she said, a resigned smile curved her mouth stiffly as she turned to face him. 'And you? Do you have kids?'

Max took a deep breath, feeling his chest tighten. He'd known it from the start she would be doggedly persistent. He should say something, tell her how dysfunctional and selfish his parents—both sets—were too. He should tell her that perhaps if he'd had better role models for parents he would not believe that he'd be a failure dad.

He should share war stories and tell her how being dumped at boarding school every Christmas was a twisted relief, sparing him from beatings or having to escape with his little sister onto the roof to distance himself from his foster parents savage drink-fueled arguments.

He could offer her some small morsel of information that might explain why he was like he was. Dangle some tiny hint before her that might help her better decipher the complex code that explained his behavior .

But he said nothing.

He had learned to block his feelings and never confide in others.

And she was a therapist.

Underestimating her could be fatal, especially to his reputation. He was a man of steel. He had the heart of a wolf. The mind of an eagle, single-minded, focused, controlled. If his competitors detected the slightest hint of weakness, the merest moral of vulnerability, the finest slither of insecurity they'd exploit it for their own commercial gain, destroying everything he'd fought so hard to maintain. He should know. He'd exploited his competitors' weaknesses in exactly that cruel, heartless fashion.

Besides his clothes spoke for him and she'd already detected the grim, funereal air to his garments.

'My kids, she said, breaking the heavy silence, 'are my children. The kids in the center,' she corrected as she turned her head, breaking their contact. She shrugged her shoulders. 'It's ironic. Sometimes I'm accused of caring too much.'

Something that felt a lot like respect tugged his chest. For some altogether odd reason in that moment it affirmed in his mind what a wonderful mother she would make, unlike—' he gripped the pen and forced his mind back to his sketch. He frowned, looking down at the chaotic weave of heavy black lines on the page.

There was no doubt about it. This woman was a troubling distraction.

10

I n just under an hour the plane began its descent. Issy pressed her nose to the window, gasping as a palatial villa appeared below them. Sitting like a jewel on top of a hill, ringed by coconut trees and exotic palms, it commanded a complex of private bures.

'Gosh, if I owned even a fingernail of that I'd never want to leave.' she said, wondering why he didn't even bother to look out the window. 'Maybe having nothing makes you appreciate it more.'

Max lifted his head briefly, grunted then bent his gaze toward his iPhone, jabbing an immaculately manicured finger at the neon screen. How he managed to hit the right buttons with those wide, strong, digits she didn't know. Neither did she know what was consuming his attention. Nor did she care personally, but she was going to make it her business. No matter how distracting he or his uber chic resort was.

As they approached the island, a modern airport with a landing strip the length of 10 football fields materialized out of the remote, hewn rock. So this is how billionaires live she thought glancing down at a staff of 20 waiting to greet them at the edge of the runway. Issy's stomach clenched then rose as the plane slid onto the tarmac. It was a fantasy world to which she could never belong.

When the plane came to a stop, the crew pushed the door open and released the stairs. The cabin flooded with the sound of a full choir rivaling that of any southern Baptist parish.

Max walked behind her at a distance, his posture stiff, as though aware of the unsettling energy that pulsed between them, as they disembarked. Which suited Issy perfectly. She was still thrown by the disconcerting effect he was having on her equilibrium. It was as though her mind and body had forsaken common sense and belonged to someone else.

She glanced at Max as a small crew approached them to unload their luggage and transport them to the villa commanding the clifftop. It was far better that he remain aloof and detached than touch her again like he'd done in the foyer of the hotel. The walls of her stomach fluttered at the heated memory.

Max remained mutely silent, the ripple of a scowl etching his tanned brow, as he hesitated before ushering her into the back of the waiting sleek black Range Rover.

A warm breeze, sweetly exotic fluttered through the open window, brushing against her skin like butterfly kisses. Yet even the unexpected sensuality couldn't melt her apprehensive mood as the convoy climbed toward the summit of the hill.

Talking about herself on the plane was one thing, getting him to open up to her and participate in her art-therapy, quite another. Issy held her breath as they approached giant wrought-iron gates guarded by a pair of massive panthers carved in black granite as if to reinforce the exclusivity of the location.

This was like Fantasy Island, she thought as the gates swung open, revealing an exotic play land. Brightly colored birds and butterflies sailed amongst lush green plants and swaying palm trees, filling the air with song.

A modern Garden of Eden, complete with all its vices, she thought looking at Max. This is not a fairy-tale, she reminded herself. This was work. And she was under no illusion that happily-ever-afters would ever be her life story. She bit her bottom lip. Hard.

Nope, Massimilliano Balforni's world wasn't her world and never would be. Her childhood memories were of mountainous family debts and frequent arguments fueled by stress. Money, she had learned, could change lives, but not always for the better. While her income was better than many working in the not-for-profit sector, she chose to pour her cash into helping kids who suffered similar hardships rather than spend it on frivolous possessions she could barely afford.

She looked down at the faded hummingbirds on her turquoise dress and tugged at the nylon fabric to stop it from clinging in all the wrong places in the sweltering heat. Even that was second-hand. Still, a girl can dream, she mused, savoring momentarily the idea that someone like her could find happiness in a place like this.

As the Range Rover stopped beneath a wide hardwood portico leading to the villa's entrance she glanced over her shoulders at the suitcases piled in the back. She had her ingredients—paints and brushes and paper...*And him*. What was she going to do with him?

'If I could bottle that scent I'd make a fortune,' Max said, his tone stripped of emotion, as he stepped from the Range Rover.

'Frangipani, sweet coconut and white musk. Fresh, yet sexy and mysterious,' he looked at her briefly, then strode up the wide terraced steps fringed with exotic plants, winding toward the large open-aired entrance.

Issy stared at him, her pulse fluttering. If I could bottle you, I'd make a fortune, she thought, vowing never to succumb to his intoxicating masculinity.

She couldn't begin to quantify how much some of her girlfriends would pay for a smidgen of time with Max Balforni. And here she was, with him all to herself on his luxurious wonderland of an island. Max the Legend, she thought making up a name she would keep only to herself.

With his chiseled dark beauty, unparalleled elegance and intelligence blending seamlessly into a powerfully masculine physique the name suited him.

There was nothing legendary about the stoic Kiwi blokes back home. Issy couldn't imagine them dressing so exquisitely, nor ever talking about how fragrant something smelled—unless it was beer, which they drank by the truckload.

This should be a dream, but it had all the hallmarks of being her worst nightmare, Issy thought as she stared at the powerful figure striding into the mansion.

Were it not for the fact Max had his iPhone

glued to his ear and the task which lay ahead she would have been entranced by the sheer beauty of the villa and luxuriant tropical garden. But she was far too anxious to think about anything other than the man she somehow had to change.

Max Balforni. Fashion magnate. Brilliantly talented, impeccably controlled, obsessively perfect, she thought while studying the manicured plants.

She stood at the entrance and waited for him to direct her to where they would be having their first session. With less than a week to complete her mission, the clock was ticking. What a success story de-stressing him would make. If she could unwind his over active mind, penetrate his fortress of a heart, rejuvenate his soul, and bring more fun and levity into his life, she could help anyone. The accolades would be huge, hopefully drawing more lucrative, highly-strung clients looking for a way to relax and reclaim their genius. This was her big chance, she reminded herself. Six days to change all their lives.

Issy plucked a Passionflower tumbling over a low stone wall near the entrance and inhaled the delicate gardenia-like aroma renowned as a natural cure for anxiety, yet not even the sweetness of the scent could shift her apprehension.

Glancing at the sprawling palatial villa, she was struck by the shocking display of wealth that oozed from every hardwood surface. It was an exotic palace beyond her wildest dreams. The entry alone was easily 40 times bigger than her own pokey little bed-sit back in New Zealand, she thought as Max signaled her to follow him inside.

She scuttled to catch up with Max as he strode inside, his phone pressed to his ear, his shoulders tense, his face impenetrable. Was it her intuition or was it fear talking, but something warned her he didn't look in the least bit interested in participating in the session she had planned.

Well, what to do? He didn't strike her as a person she could order to take part in her program. That never worked with kids, and it sure wouldn't work with him. She could slow the pace a little, try the tortoise and the hare method. It's not who gets there fastest but who wins the race, she thought trailing after him.

The house is a reflection of self, she had heard once. Her heart skipped a beat, beginning to relish the challenge. She would take a little time settling into things and see what Max Balforni's environment would reveal. After all, it was only early morning, and they had the rest of the day.

'You're so lucky.' Issy sighed, 'This has to be the most beautiful place in the universe.' She beamed an extra wide sunny smile, sensing like an eagle if he detected the slightest sign of weakness he would circle for the kill.

11

———

Her comment was met with stony silence. Not a muscle in his hard, handsome face moved as she strode ahead. Max's walk was purposeful with a controlled, yet impatient, strength to it as he led her through the villa. Clearly, he was in a hurry to be rid of her.

Issy slowed her pace deliberately, gasping audibly as she walked past walls lined with priceless artworks she'd only ever seen in borrowed books and on the Internet.

'This place is like a museum. It's immaculate,' Issy said, as she followed him past a living room double the size of a luxury-hotel lobby, opening out to a massive wrap-around deck with panoramic views of the sea. The vibrant turquoise hues of the ocean spreading below contrasted with the starkness of Max's mood. 'You must love coming here,' she ventured.

'I don't have time for holidays,' he said. 'I have full-time staff to ensure it is available all year round for friends or family who may want to relax,' his tone was flat as though the thought of chilling surrounded by so much beauty didn't excite him one little bit.

His footsteps were silent on the smooth marble floor, contrasting with her sandals clacking noisily as she quickened her pace to keep up with him. Friends with benefits no doubt, Issy thought. She didn't know a stitch about his love life but she didn't have to be a NASA scientist to guess that a man as handsome and wealthy as Max would be inundated with beautiful women offering their services.

Suddenly she froze, her heart pounding, as they walked down a glass paneled hallway toward a painting as small as the Mona Lisa.

'Oh, my gosh,' Issy's breathing raced as she stepped closer, her nose almost pressed against the canvas as she traced every ethereal brush stroke. 'Is that a Morandi?' she gasped, her voice a high-pitched whisper. To anyone else the painting would just be a collection of ordinary objects—bottles and jars standing stoically against a muted background, but in the hands of a master even the ordinary could be elevated to transcendent beauty—and equally as potent.

Max's grave mood lifted as his eyes followed the source of her attraction. He touched his mouth, drawing attention to his sensuous lips as he nodded.

She gasped, mentally computing a painting of this worth was beyond anything she would ever experience up close in her lifetime. Her heart hammered with equal measures of thrill and fear, as though at any moment a security guard would command her to step back beyond the rail, or escort her from the house, except there was no barrier rail. And for the next few days at least, this house of treasure would be her home.

Rummaging in her bag, she whipped out her camera 'May I take a photo?'

His gaze narrowed as his dark, fierce eyes riveted to her. He nodded. 'Paintings should be appreciated.'

She took several photos then turned to him. 'Gosh, this is like being in an art museum. We'll never see paintings like this in New Zealand, and there's no way I'll ever get to Europe, not on my wage.' Startled by the strange glint in his eye, she threw her attention back to the painting again.

'It's true when they say his paintings can transport you. Like you could fold into them and escape reality.' Nothing she was feeling was even close to reality, she thought achingly aware of her energy pulsing in tiny quivers toward Max as she stood in front of him. Not a muscle in his body moved as he stood like concrete, his broad shoulders rigid, his posture stiff, yet she sensed he felt the magnetic energy pulse between them too.

It was as if Morandi had infused the bottles with an aura-like energy, which seeped from the painting blanketing them both.

Max stood like a sentry, slightly at a distance, behind her like the stoic blue-black bottle and the fine white vase in the painting, touching but not touching.

He turned to her, his normally cool blue eyes now a penetrating black. 'Is beauty the bringing together of opposites to make one?'

His unexpected question threw her. Whether he was speaking of the white and black bottles in the painting, or of their own obvious differences she didn't know, but she found herself wishing recklessly it was the latter.

'Opposites attract,' she ventured, her voice catching as she watched the sunlight glance off his waves of dark hair, then move across the surface of his face, tracing the muscular lines of his strong cheekbones, the indentations of his dimples, before settling on the black-silk-like fiber clinging to his powerful chest. 'There must be a reason for that.'

She forced a laugh, noticing with alarm that it sounded more nervous than confident.

There was a reason why the energy sparked and cracked and hissed between them. A reason she would never, could never, explore. 'I know Morandi believed finding beauty in opposition would create a happier world,' she said, steering the conversation to safer ground.

'You are well informed.' His eyes glistened with vitality as though he was both surprised and impressed with her level of knowledge.

'Actually, I studied art history at college, briefly,' she said, softly. 'Something my parents reluctantly indulged. I remember being captivated by Morandi's work, one of Italy's finest still life painters, but I never in a zillion years thought I'd ever see the real thing.'

'You said, "briefly"' he paused, inviting her to go on.

Issy hesitated, aware that he was asking all the questions, and once again she was hogging the ear time when really the roles should be reversed. But perhaps in the sharing of what appeared to be a mutual passion she might learn a little about him. It would be the only passion they could share, she thought, willing her throbbing pulse to slow.

'I was at college, young and dependent on my parents, we needed money. Art wasn't an indulgence we could afford.' Issy's chest felt tight as she relived a part of her childhood she preferred to forget. 'There's no money in art, they told me. Get a real job. Keep it as a hobby, blah, blah, blah.'

She forced a smile as she looked at the painting, 'It's ironic when you realize how much money these artists earned when they followed their passion. But anyway, it was what it was. And I wanted to please them. So, as you know, I went and trained as a clinical psychologist.' She shook her head and gave a humorless laugh. 'I thought it might help me figure out my dysfunctional family.'

Max studied her intensely, the gleam in his eyes acknowledging her disillusionment. 'Perhaps I should have studied psychology too,' he said, a weariness in his tone that came not just from tiredness, but from life. 'But now you're an art therapist. It is difficult to remain true to yourself and your philosophy. I respect that.'

There he was complimenting her again. His tone was so earnest Issy felt herself blush. Being understood and appreciated felt too good. And too foreign. And that was the problem she thought helplessly. Talking like this was merging the personal and the professional together dangerously. Two forces in opposition like oil and water which a sane person, a professional person, knew would never mix.

Only she wasn't sane, she acknowledged. Not anymore. Not with him being so kind. Not with those sexy dimples indenting as his lips curved into a kind smile. It was easier to keep her distance when he was aloof and remote.

She looked away, knowing she must dismiss his comment as politeness not interest in her for fear of wanting something that would never be hers.

Him.

Cultured people like Max were raised to be polite and she mustn't let herself think he was in the slightest bit interested in who she was as a person. But he was a good listener, and as rare as it was for someone to focus on her for a change it felt nice. She could share how art made her feel, find out what moved him and still maintain a professional distance.

'It's incredible how a painting can affect you,' she said. 'It's completely out of your control. My heart is racing, the hairs on my arms are tingling like crazy. I feel inspired and breathless, and light headed,' she said. It was the painting, not him, definitely not him that was creating all these crazy physical sensations, she thought, surprised by the powerful emotions cascading through her.

'Can you believe, my eyes are pooling, like at any moment I might cry. You know, it's almost like the feeling you have when you're in love. Is that why you purchased this painting?' she said.

His eyes focused on her with razor-like intensity, sending shivers racing up her spine.

'Art is not about emotion. Art is about power.' His head jerked backward sharply.

'Oh, yes,' she said, pleased that on this point they agreed. 'The power of art, as Picasso once said, to wash from the soul the dust of everyday life.'

His lips twisted in a wry smile. 'You are a romantic Ms. Riley. It is very sweet. But also naïve. The power of art, Ms Riley, is about money. Possessing what others covet and can never afford.'

Issy felt blood roar through her chest as she looked at the imposing man standing beside her. 'No! Art is about feeling.'

'You know, I actually think you believe that nonsense,' he interjected. Max stepped toward her, encroaching upon her physical space until they were both nearly touching like the bottles in the painting.

Issy stood her ground, lifting her chin toward him as he stood over her. Was he really so emotionally blocked that he could feel nothing? 'What happened to make you so unfeeling, so hard, so cynical?'

'Life, Miss Riley. Life.'

'Don't you believe in love?'

'Love,' he grimaced, staring at the cold blue

bottle in the painting, 'is a business construct manufactured by salesmen and marketers to manipulate people like you.'

'Have you always been so cynical?' Issy challenged. 'Love is a feeling. Like art is a feeling,' she shrugged. 'It's hard to describe in words, but you know it when you sense it. It's a warm, fantastic, life-giving feeling. Like eating ice-cream in summer, only without the calories.'

'A feeling,' Max snorted. 'Another vague, nebulous, overused concept. I love that dress. I love those shoes. I love that painting.' He turned toward her, looking directly into her eyes as though laying down a challenge.

'I love you.' His words delivered with icy hard detachment splintered through the warm air. His head jerked back sharply, 'See how easy it is to say?'

He sounded cold, far more bitter than she'd expected, but something about the way Max strode stiffly toward the edge of the deck and stood gazing out at the blue sea, a pensive frown on those beautiful dark brows, made her wonder if perhaps even he thought he'd gone too far.

'Show me a love that lasts,' he said, turning to her at last.

What could she say? She'd notched up her Guinness Book record of impermanent affairs of the heart, the canceled wedding her most public failure.

But she wouldn't tell him that. Not yet. Not ever. She could barely bring herself to talk about it with anyone, let alone a client she hoped to impress with her togetherness.

'So we agree on something,' Max said, filling the silent vacuum, 'I've never felt it, never found it, never fantasized about it and I never will. Feeling is a distraction I can't afford.'

'Who did that to you?' She said, wondering how a man who seemed to have everything, had so little.

Max flinched, his jaw hardening in steely resolve. 'I'm a realist.'

'If you don't have love,' Issy pressed, 'or at least the hope of love, what do you have?' She stepped toward him, concern widening her eyes.'Max?' she whispered, probing for his reply

'Work. I have work. Now if you'll excuse me I'll take you to your private bure. I'm sure you'll find the peninsular villa to your liking. You won't be disturbed. I only ask that you show me the same courtesy.'

Adrenaline spiked in her chest. He was banishing her. 'But what about the session I have planned for today?'

12

'This art-therapy thing—it's just not me,' Max said, as they strolled toward the peninsular villa, winding past tropical flowers and swaying palms, opening onto sudden vistas of pristine white beaches.

'Then why am I here?' Issy said, fixing him with a piercing gaze that told him she'd anticipated his resistance.

'If you're like most women you'll enjoy an all-expenses paid holiday,' he said, quickening his pace.

'I always pay my own way, Mr. Balforni. And while a holiday would be nice we both know that's not why I'm here. You say art therapy isn't you, and yet you've never tried it. Do you always judge things so prematurely?'

Max's brows knitted together. He never made

any decisions without a thorough analysis of the outcomes, but clearly he had under-estimated her work ethic. While the trait was an admirable one, he had no intention of submitting to her plans. Nor did he intend to string her along. Above all else, even to his detriment, he was honest. The prospect of a week of pretense gnawed at his conscience.

'I am sure you are very good at what you do—'

'*But,*' she interrupted, 'I can hear your 'but." A balmy breeze lifted a tendril of her hair as her lips curved in a warm, understanding smile that threatened to melt his resistance. It wasn't the practiced smile of a catwalk model, but one which infused her whole presence, settling in her far too innocent eyes, eyes that could see right through to his soul.

Being near her was definitely a bad idea, he thought, fortifying his resolve as Issy plucked a flower from a bush of hibiscus and tucked it behind her hair. She may look like an innocent but he was under no illusion why she was there.

She would fail in her task to mine the depths of his emotions, he would ensure that. 'Look I don't know what you've been told, or what you hope to achieve, but I can assure you your talents would be better employed elsewhere,' he said. 'Besides it's Christmas. Wouldn't you rather be home with your family?'

'Honestly?' she said, her eyes trailing off into the

distance. 'No. Why would I subject myself to their disapproval when I can stay here in paradise? Besides, the terms of my contract are clear. Six days.'

'*Bene.*Be my guest. There is plenty to do and you will have the place to yourself. Do you play golf—we have an 18 hole course?

Issy shook her head, 'No can do.'

'Do you eat? There's five restaurants, all with Michelin chefs.'

'I'm not hungry.'

'Diving?'

'Nope.'

'Well, then I'm sure you'll find plenty to enjoy at the spa.'

'Look,' she said, striding up to him. 'I'm not here on a junket. I've been contracted to provide a service. One I intend to deliver. Six days of art therapy.'

'Finger painting is not my thing.'

Issy stopped suddenly on the edge of the peninsula, thrusting her hands on her hips as she waited for him to face her. 'I can't force you to participate, but if it's any comfort it's normal to feel a bit fearful.'

'*Scuse?*'

'Trying anything for the first time can feel strange,' Issy said,'especially delving into the subconscious. Sometimes people are afraid to let go and see what unfolds.'

No one talked to him like that. *Ever.* But rather

than irritate him, he found himself relishing the banter. 'Fear, Ms. Riley is not in my vocabulary.'

'Please call me Issy.'

'Issy.' Her name slipped too easily from his tongue, felt too pleasing, too soft, too treacherous.

'Maybe you think anything I have to offer is beneath you.' Her green eyes glittered with a proud savagery that ignited something primal deep inside him. She would not pander to his mood, nor pretend something she did not feel. Dare he admit it but the novelty of the challenge verged on enjoyable. And he respected her blistering honesty.

'If you're so dead against participating why don't you just climb back into your plane and high fly it out of here?' She flung her hands out toward the sea.

Max thrust his shoulders back, tilting his chin. Her challenge, inferring that he would even contemplate fleeing, only made his decision more resolute. Did she have any idea of the insult she'd just offered? If there was one thing he would never do, it was run. While he detested emotional weakness, he was also a red-blooded male in his prime, a man who relished the role of being the hunter, not the prey.

'I will not be leaving. I gave my word' he said, sharply.

'You don't seem like the sort of man who does anything he doesn't want.'

'My promise once given is never broken,' he snapped.

Issy's eyes glistened as though something he had said had hit a potent note. 'If only more men were promise keepers', she said softly.

The echo of sadness in her voice sharpened his senses. Why was she hiding away on an island in the middle of nowhere trying to help him with his own emotions, when he sensed it was her that clearly needed healing?

She was so close he could almost reach out and comfort her. She was so near he could almost feel the warmth of her too soft skin. She was so damned innocent.

Too damned desirable.

'Max—'

Competing emotions battled in Max's gut. A shudder of carnal pleasure at the sound of his name slipping from her lips unavoidably led him to imagine her calling out his name in the throes of passion, followed by disquiet at the feelings she incited in him and annoyance that she saw herself as some sort of rescuer.

It had been a mistake to pander to his sister's fears about his health. And the persistent woman standing before him now was wrong, it wasn't the past he feared but the future.

'Are you Okay?' she whispered, concern pooling

in her eyes as he stood rigid and motionless before her.

'Nothing is wrong,' he said, half in truth and half a lie. Why did someone so wrong feel so, so terrifyingly right?

'Oh, I get it now,' she said. 'You promised to bring me to the island but you didn't promise to participate or spend any time with me,' Issy shook her head. 'You've brought me here on pretense. First the fake name, and now this. Where will the lies stop?' Her cheeks flushed, not from irritation but something more painful—some hurt that struck at Max's frozen heart.

Why did he suddenly feel guilty? He stole a glance at Issy as she gazed out to sea. Sunlight glinted off her hair throwing golden highlights through the blaze of pink like a sunset. Her eyes glittered with a blend of heat and something else he couldn't quite put his finger on, giving her a delectably innocent pre-Raphaelite glow, as she turned to him.

A primal need surged in his loins. There were worse ways to spend a week.

'Have dinner with me,' he commanded.

13

Think work. Business. And for God's sake don't rip this dress. Issy picked up the fine silk evening dress Max had asked her to wear. Sprinkled with a shimmer of beige-gold sequin flowers with a long elegant fish-tale, it looked like a dress belonging to a mermaid. Her hands trembled. Did Max really trust her to wear something so expensive?

Trailing her fingers over the cool silken fibers, she glanced back at her own dress, lying in a shapeless heap where she'd tossed it on her bed. Max was right, the natural fibers of silk felt far more refreshing than the cheap synthetic fabric of her own clothes. Nylon made her feel like she was wearing a plastic supermarket bag. And while she'd been drawn to the bright colors she had to concede most of her clothes were impractical in Fiji's sultry heat.

All day she'd soaked up all the humidity, exploring his estate while he skillfully evaded her, God knows where. But tonight, she thought, picking up the dress, she'd make sure he didn't want to avoid her again.

As the dress slipped over her body painful anticipation brought heat to her skin and she recalled the silken touch of Max's hand as he'd handed her back her knickers in the lobby.

Don't be a fool, she admonished, as a desire she didn't dare consider coiled through the air. Ever since she'd met him he'd been a perfect gentleman. Proof again that he was no more interested in her than she was in having a Fiji fling.

Which was reassuring. Wasn't it?

Why, then, was she worried about making a good impression? And not just a good business impression. Because it had never mattered before. Until tonight Issy hadn't wanted to impress any man enough to worry whether she looked or felt sexy.

Dare she admit it, she thought as she walked across the room, the dress made her feel like a princess. Powerful, aristocratic, and beautiful.

Beautiful.

She studied herself in the reflection shimmering off the floor-length panoramic window. No, that was taking it a bit too far. Her mother would have said she looked like a second class Cinderella.

Issy pulled her shoulders back and took a deep breath. She preferred to think she was dressing for a part she was required to play. If she wanted to understand Max better she needed to be part of his world.

She looked down at her boobs only just contained by the plunging neckline caught in a gorgeous sapphire clasp at her waist. The only requirement she decided was that there be no sign of cleavage anywhere.

She hoisted up the straps, then covered her upper body with the silk chiffon wrap he'd left in her room. Strangely, she actually felt good, a little wild maybe, but intoxicatingly free. Although the colors were more subdued than she would normally wear, the neutral tones accented her green eyes and made her skin glow.

Surely Max wouldn't notice she felt way out of her depth.Now, what to put on her long, narrow feet? Her yellow Crocs would look ghastly, worse they'd make her look matriarchal.

Issy settled on the gold strappy sandals he'd sent to her room. That Max managed to know her exact size she put down to years of experience dressing supermodels, rather than a specific interest in her personally.

What surprised her more was that, in a fashion world renown for dressing stick-insects, he had anything in her size at all. She pressed her hand against her stomach, suppressing a flutter of wayward warmth.

Now, what to do with her face, she thought as she walked to the bathroom. While she didn't want to go the whole hog with girly make up the dress deserved better.

Staring at the freckles marching a confident line over her nose and cheeks, she decided she wouldn't cover them up with foundation like his flawless supermodel girlfriends obviously did. While she'd do her best to fit into his world, she would still retain some measure of authenticity.

She thumbed through her lipsticks and settled on a soft, barely-there shade of raisin called Kiss Me Twice, a similar hue to the sequins on her dress. Her stomach fluttered like tiny butterflies as she drew a painted line along her lips.

Max would not be kissing her twice, not even once, she reminded herself forcing herself to refocus on the whole point of making a special effort.

Issy blotted the lipstick, removing any excess. She would downplay her lips. Lips that *must not*, did not, long for a kiss. Instead, she would accentuate her best feature, and hopefully her most hypnotic feature. Her eyes.

Normally she used muted browns, but the occasion demanded more glamor. Opting to create an aubergine smoky eye to add a layer of intrigue Issy smoothed a creamy lavender eye shadow all over the lid, up to the brow. Then applied a deeper creamy purple shadow into the crease, and blended it up and out emphasizing the contours of the al-mond shape of her eyes.

It was amazing how the color picked up the vi-olet and gold highlights around her irises, she thought, sweeping on two generous coats of black mascara. After blending a creamy plum-coloured blush onto the apples of the cheeks she decided she was done.

Wow! She exclaimed, surprising herself at the transformation. The effect was pure alchemy. She looked like an eclectic blend of wild feline and mes-merizing mermaid. Not bad, she thought uncharac-teristically, enjoying turning her face into a canvas for what she hoped would be a hypnotic effect.

All she had to do to get him to open up was to distract him. But not with her boobs, boobs were definitely off the agenda.

Issy frowned as self-doubt rose in her conscious-ness. Even the soft sheen to her lips looked—

Looked—

Well, slightly provocative.

Was the whole effort too try-hard?

Her mother's voice wormed through the humid air as Issy walked toward the door. *Don't box above your weight.* She turned back, seized by a painful sense of her own shortcomings. Was she just about to make a fool of herself? Would Max take one look at her with eyes that savored perfection and realize that she'd gone to a lot of trouble to make herself look like she belonged? Would he miss the point that her motivation wasn't glamor but empowerment?

Issy hesitated. Then took a deep breath. Throwing her shoulders back, and drawing the wrap tightly around her, she wandered out to the garden. She took the path along the side of the pool toward the dining area, hoping the serenity of the water and the gentle rustling of the willowy palms would calm the erratic pounding of her heart.

Sorry to disappoint you *again,* Mum.

14

From the thatched deck of the private dining cantilevered above the lagoon, Max watched Issy stride into sight, tall and lithe and stepping with the sure footedness of a goddess.

Her full hips and long legs emphasized the seductive curves of her womanly body as she walked. Hair the color of rose gold bounced playfully in the balmy breeze to reveal the bewitching contours of her innocent face, while the golden light of the fading sun played like a halo around her.

A beguiling goddess he decided—more Aphrodite than the warrior Athena. But while he had always preferred the challenge of intelligence to rampant insatiable sexuality, something about the way she married the two stirred life inside him, a primal instinct that threw him.

Gripping the edge of the railing he vowed not to succumb to temptation. Hadn't Eve dazzled Adam with the same playful innocence, he thought, unable to tear his eyes away from her as she drew closer toward him.

Max knew better than most that appearances were not facts. Caring types, like counselors and psychologists, were skilled at cultivating trust.

Whatever feelings of attraction he felt were no doubt par for the course. But acting on those traitorous feelings would be foolish. He was here to extricate himself from the entanglements of his life.

Besides he'd known from their first meeting she wasn't a suitable candidate for a sexual conquest. Apart from the fact she was technically his employee, she simply wasn't his type; she was an outsider. A refreshingly down to earth one who exuded a simple, uncomplicated innocence that hinted at a charming naivety.

Maybe.

But she was far too comfortable inhabiting a domain that he would never be comfortable exploring. Emotions.

Whatever her agenda, she was proving to be quite the chameleon. Morphing from poolside mayhem to lagoon nymph, he mused, studying the sway of the silk and sequin dress as it clung to her curves. The pleasure he felt, Max told himself, was the heightened satisfaction he'd felt when he'd been the first designer to champion fashion for fuller figure women, not the anorexic, wash-board women his industry immorally perpetuated.

Real women with curves, like the goddess advancing toward him now. He watched mesmerized as she paused momentarily to gaze up at the full moon. The silk shawl she languidly wrapped around her slipped from her shoulders, revealing the creamy, full swell of her breasts. To his consternation Max found himself smiling.

Heat flared in his loins. *Damn, he wanted her.* He raked his fingers through his hair, then massaged his temples, striving with limited success for control. He wanted her but he would never act on it. His work was his mistress. There would be no other.

Issy turned and looked up at him, her eyes widening in bewilderment as though sensing is turmoil. His heart jack-knifed then hammered as their eyes locked. For a brief irrational moment, it was as if they shared a connection uniting them through time and space.

Preposterous, he muttered, striding across the deck. The whole thing was illogical. Whatever happened, one thing was certain, emotion could not control, nor cloud, his mind.

Issy hesitated and glanced back at the path she'd just followed as though contemplating turning back, then wrapping her shawl tightly around her, came toward him.

Max drew a ragged breath. The image of a fatal seductress beguiling him with her innocence coiled again like a mirage through the heated twilight haze.

Instead of the unsophisticated disarmingly plain woman he had known her to be she now oozed a potent physical radiance of which she seemed strangely unaware. This is madness, he told himself. Quelling the slow growl of sexual hunger in his loins, he greeted her coolly.

'*Buona Sera.*'

'Good evening,' she said softly

'The dress looks nice,' he said, with cold detachment. Nice? What the hell was he thinking? Nice. He didn't do nice. Nice was such a mediocre word. But he couldn't very well tell her the truth. "You look devastatingly beautiful. You set my loins ablaze. You set every fiber in my body on fire." His fingers throbbed with the need to touch.

'It's a beautiful dress,' she murmured. 'Thank you for allowing me to wear it.'

'It suits you well.' *Too well.* He thrust his hands in his pockets.

She blushed like a new bride. Something about her innocence excited him. Keeping his face impassive, he walked to the table and pulled out her chair.

'May I take your wrap?'

She hesitated, oddly reluctant to surrender her cover. She needn't have worried, the silk of her shawl was too thin to do a half-way decent job of covering her breasts.

'Thank you.' She painted a strained smile on her lips, as though manifesting a confidence he sensed she didn't feel.

His arousal instantly banished, replaced instead by a desire to protect her from harm. Harm he knew too well he was capable of unintentionally inflicting. He would hurt her —like he hurt them all. Women always wanted more from him than he was able to give. Only this time, for some reason he couldn't fathom, it really mattered.

15

The Universe seemed to freeze, suspending them in a fragile bubble of silence and intimacy, as strong sensual hands lightly touched her shoulders, sending shudders through Issy's body. She drew a ragged breath, inhaling the earthy scent of Max's cologne, as he lifted the wrap from her. His fingers brushed her neck, sending tremors scuttling down her spine.

Get a grip she cautioned, while her body dreamed a wish she didn't dare desire. Of course, he didn't want her. *Not like that.* Any sensuality implied by his touch was purely accidental.

But why did he look at her with eyes that seemed to undress her? He was just obsessed with his design she told herself as he studied her with such intensity that Issy squirmed in her seat. No doubt it was an occupational habit. A career built dressing glamorous woman was certain to have its distinct advantages. What goes on must come off, right?

It would be premature to say he enjoyed breaking hearts, she knew little of his personal life, but it was no doubt an arena in which he was accomplished. Yet, now despite all the hazard lights flashing in her mind, she couldn't stop staring at him too; mesmerized by his looks, succumbing to his charm, captivated by his charisma. *Hook, line and lead sinker.*

He moved with the controlled fluidity of a Navy Seal as he walked around the table, his body taut but supple, strong yet lithe, and lethally sexy.

As he took his seat opposite her something shockingly hot and turbulent churned inside Issy's stomach. She fixed her gaze on the crystal glasses sparkling in the candlelight on the white damask tablecloth, and the silver cutlery richly burnished by the gentle flames.

The staff had obviously gone to a lot of trouble. The place looked fit for a wedding. She felt a sharp jolt in her chest and placed her right hand over her left, gripping the finger where her wedding ring would have been.

"Breathe," she affirmed silently, inhaling the softly intimate perfume of the gardenias and frangipani's arranged in an elegant vase to settle her nerves. "Breathe."

Max lifted a large black bottle, with an embossed gold label written with flourishes of French from the decanter. 'Champagne?' His voice vibrated through her body like a violin concerto. That damned voice that always made her knees go weak. Why couldn't he have a voice like a foghorn, rather than that far too sexy, almost hypnotic voice? And as for the setting, she thought, gazing out at the full moon shimmering upon the lagoon, being in paradise wasn't helping one little bit.

'Champagne?' he asked again, bringing her back to the present.

She hesitated. It had been a year since she'd last had a drink. Trying to fix her betrayed heart by drowning it in alcohol had been a fool's strategy. But her heart wasn't broken anymore and it seemed silly to refuse. The champers was obviously expensive, and she was curious to know what millionaire bubbles tasted like. Besides what harm could one weeny glass do?

'Cheers, thanks,' she said, momentarily forgetting that she wasn't having a round at the local pub with her mates.

Max's lips curved in a bemused smile as he nodded to one of the staff hovering discreetly in the shadows.

'Red champagne? Isn't that unusual?' Issy exclaimed as burgundy bubbles foamed into the crystal glass and sparkled up to the rim.

'Extraordinarily rare,' Max said, raising his glass in a toast. 'Just like the situation we both find ourselves in.'

She held her breath, trying to keep her trembling hand steady, and prayed the bubbles wouldn't land with an undignified splash on his expensive dress.

'Yes,' she said, taking a small sip before placing the glass down. 'I'm here to help you and you keep avoiding me,' she smiled tightly, hoping she didn't sound confrontational, and then laughed. 'But then in my line of work that's not so rare.'

'How so?' He said, sipping from his glass.

'It's always like that when concerned others sign their loved ones up for therapy. It's as though they come pre-programmed to refuse help.'

Max took a gulp of champagne, swishing it slowly in his mouth, as though savoring her claim. Issy, tucked her hair behind her ears several times as they sat in an uneasy silence.

'So, how was your day?' she said, after more awkward silence. Okay, so it wasn't brain surgeon conversation, but she was determined to keep her mind away from the traitorous feelings her body continued to brew as her eyes met his. The catch was she didn't want to. But what she did want to know was what he had been doing all day and just when exactly her client intended on participating in her sessions.

Max sat motionless, his poker face reinforcing he wasn't about to divulge anything easily. So she would have to take her time, rather than rush him.

'Okay. That's cool. It's all good. Let's talk about something you do like then—fashion,'

'I don't like to talk about it. I speak through my clothes.'

'Really? Then what does this dress say?' she asked, rising from her chair and turning with deliberately slow movements to allow him to savor it from every angle. It was licentious of her but what else did she have right now to compel him to cede control. She turned again to face him.

Beneath the rich licorice-black hair, his face had lost color, the brilliant sapphire-blue flecks in his eyes standing out dramatically against the pallor of his cheeks.

'Okay, let me intuit,' she said, strangely empowered by his uncomfortable silence. 'I'm guessing if this dress could speak it would say, "Why am I here?" She walked to the edge of the room as smoothly and elegantly as she could, blazingly aware his eyes were riveted to her.

'"What am I doing on this remote island?"' she

said, waving her arm out toward the open sea humming in rhythmic waves below them, "Isolated from anything remotely familiar.'" She spun to face him. 'All the other dresses, the ones filling the racks you have in your study, well, they're wondering the same thing too.'

His eyes were wary. His body had the stillness of a wild animal whose every sense was alert, suspicious and untrusting.

'I see you've wasted no time busying yourself with my affairs,' he gritted out. The crack of his anger was nearly audible.

'You said, "feel free to explore." So I did, and I discovered your studio—quite by chance,' she held his gaze, refusing to flinch under the weight of his obvious displeasure. 'Why, when you're not supposed to be working, have you brought your collection?' she challenged.

'I've made no secret that I've no intention of abandoning my work. However, I will concede,' he said, his tone slowing to a low, sensuous crawl, 'increasingly I think allowing myself a little distraction may prove therapeutic, *mia tentatrice*.'

Something about the way his eyes trailed along her throat before resting on the swell of her breasts, implied he intended to unsettle her and seize back control. It affirmed her earlier conviction that he thought he could have her if he wanted, flushing color to her cheeks. Why did he invade her psyche like this? Why did she go weak at the kneecaps whenever he was near? Why did she feel he had far more control over her than she did?

Issy felt her chest flame. She was playing with fire. What had she been thinking? He was the consummate control freak and she was way out of her depth. 'We're lucky with the weather,' she said noticing with horror that her voice rather than sounding bright and nonchalant throbbed with frisky sexiness. What's wrong with you? She berated herself.

'I was told that Christmas is the rainy season,' her husky tone subsided into a squeak, as she took her seat. 'The forecasters are saying this will be the driest one on record.' she said, instantly regretting the banality of her conversation.

She sighed with relief as the Fijian waiting staff walked toward them carrying platters piled high with lobster and oysters and other assorted seafood dishes.

'Are you hungry?' he asked, his sultry tone ambiguous.

'Ravenous.' Her eyes locked on his sensuous lips. Lips that could command a legion of Templar Knights by day and by night plunder the depths of a woman's body. Good grief what was she thinking?

She was relieved when he began questioning her about her techniques and what drew her to her work as they ate their meal. The conversation led to her wider interest in art and Issy found herself settling into something curiously like comfort.

For some reason, they were just staring into each other's eyes and talking. To her astonishment, she also found that both liked expressionism, particularly the works of Matisse, Rothko, and Kandinsky, artists known more for their spirituality and emotional expression than other artists. And, even more surprisingly a shared sense of humor. Her stomach churned. It was all quite unnerving.

'Have you lost your appetite?' Max's voice brought her thoughts back to the 1/2 eaten lobster on her plate.

'Um...' she stammered, 'I'm not really hungry,' she said, weakly. She felt dizzy, her senses heightened, every hair on her body standing alert, almost like she'd experienced standing in front of the Morandi. No. The idea was absurd, a fantasy, a prospect as unpalatable as it was dangerous.

No, she affirmed silently, she was strictly in love with the setting, the place. Not him and the fantasy of the life he inhabited, a fantasy that would only end in tears.

'I've thoroughly enjoyed the evening. It's been awesome. Pretty surreal in fact, and the dress, what can I say—the dress says it all. Glamor, allure, enchantment. Being a model for Emporio Balforni— sheer fantasy. Fun though too. This is like a fairytale, being here—with you, except as you know, I'm here to work. And it's late. If I don't get back to my bure now, I'm afraid I may just turn into a pumpkin.'

'You are working. You are helping with my collection. And I find your company refreshing.'

Why was he being so damned charming? 'I'm glad. You'll find our sessions tomorrow refreshing too,' she said, 'We've got an early start. To catch up on the time we missed today,' she said, hoping she sounded convincingly assured he would agree to participate. 'Would you think it rude of me if I went to—'

Don't say bed. Don't even think bed. '—Would you mind if I retired?' she forced her voice to a nonchalant crawl.

'*Va bene*. Of course,' Max rose to his feet. 'I will accompany you to your room.'

'No,' she said far too quickly. 'I mean, well, it's all good. I can make my own way. Really, I don't want to be a bother.' What she really wanted to say was, "actually I'm in a spot of bother, and it's all about you, so it would be better if I just went to my room, took a cold shower, and went to bed."

'One of the few things my father did do well was teach us impeccable manners, *principessa,*' he said, walking behind her chair and pulling it out as she rose to her feet.

Something in his tone evoked empathy. Once again reminding her that perhaps she wasn't the only one with a dysfunctional family. She held his gaze for a moment hoping he'd elaborate.

'Are you well *principessa*, you look flushed?'

Flushed didn't cut it. Try, on fire.

'I'm fine,' she swallowed and pinned a small, desperate smile to her lips.'Honestly. My face always goes red when I drink expensive wine.'

'*Allora*. Okay. Time for bed.'

A molten undercurrent of anticipation robbed her voice of sobriety. 'Okay,' she squeaked breathlessly.

'WELL THIS IS ME,' she said, as they walked along the torch-lined path toward her bure.

His muscular body gleamed in the torchlight as he stood in the door way, not moving except for his chest which rose and fell fast beneath the crisp cotton of his shirt. Silhouetted against the night, his jaw shadowed, his pupils huge, planting his feet firmly on the ground as though he was wrestling with an urge he refused to allow.

The subtle aroma of his cologne mixed with the scent of the tropical air made her swoon.

Issy opened the door super slowly, wishing the night would never end. Wishing for the most reckless moment that she would not spend the night alone. 'Goodnight,' she whispered.

'*Buona notte*,' he said, smiling at her oddly.

She stepped inside, shutting the door behind her so quickly that she nearly jammed the edge of her dress. It was the romantic setting, she thought firmly, not the desire to spend the night with a man she could never have. She stared toward the majestic bed bathed in the moonlight streaming through the louvered shutters. She'd be inhuman if she didn't dream of a little romance. And she'd be lying if she denied that a kiss wouldn't make the night a 10 out of 10 in any girl's book.

She braced herself against the back of the door, fighting against the urge to fling it open. Like a clichéd scene from a romantic movie, she wondered if Max was waiting for her. *Monkey mind*, she muttered under her breath. Her creativity was in equal parts strength and curse, imagining, as she was now, a future that would never be hers. She wanted him,

but she could never have him. She would always be
the hired help.

Issy felt for the light switch and flicked it on. She
froze, wide-eyed, barely breathing. 'Oh, my gosh,'
she gasped, as she followed the beam of light illuminating the Morandi painting she'd admired, now
hanging over the bed. Was that why he was acting
so oddly as they said good night? Was he hoping to
see how she reacted?

Impulsively she ran to the door, flung it open,
and ran down the path toward him as he strode past
the pool. 'I can't believe you did that for me.'

He turned, a faint smile curving his lips.

'I'm going to cry,' she flung her arms around his
shoulders, squeezing his powerful frame in what
should have been an innocuous hug. She felt his
muscles stiffen, then every cell in his body pulse as
his heated chest press against hers.

17

A *hug.*

    His family weren't huggers, a childhood of neglect had instilled that, Max thought grimly. Hugs made one weak, vulnerable, craving attachments that never lasted. No woman had ever hugged him.

Not like that.

Not a hug that was as warm, affectionate, and loving, as it was dangerously addictive.

Max felt his shoulders tense as Issy coiled her arms around his waist, then felt a fiery haze of blind lust bolt through him as her warm, soft breasts pressed against his chest.

His nostrils filled with the scent of the wild jasmine and frangipani scented toiletries he'd left in the guest bure as he took a ragged breath. On anyone else the perfume would be harmless, but on Issy it was an aphrodisiac he felt powerless to fight.

The night sky was awash with thousands of stars glinting off her rippling waves of hair, weaving a spell that for some impulsive reason made him kiss the top of her head.

'That was so kind,' she stammered, dropping trembling hands. 'The painting, I mean.'

She was such an innocent, so refreshingly un-spoiled, so authentically real Max thought as she gazed up at him with those infinite eyes, now wide and starry. He should have stepped away and broken the trance but instead, he lifted a whisper of hair tumbling over those long bewitching lashes and tucked it behind her ear.

If only she hadn't lifted her face to his. If only she hadn't parted those perfect lips. If only she was like all the other women he knew. Aloof, over-confi-dent, sterile in their botoxed perfectness.

But Issy was none of these, he thought, wrestling for control. Her hair smelled too good, her skin felt too soft and tasty. She was an elixir, an antidote, a cure to all that was fake, wrong and harsh in the world.

Suddenly, unable to fight any longer, he wanted to taste all she had to offer. Greedily, with the hunger of a man with no restraint, no self-control, no thought of anyone but his desire to taste her forbidden fruit, his lips sought the softness of her neck, the smooth curves of her cheek, then plundered her sensuous lips.

He heard a tiny gasp.

Max felt her feeble resistance as she tried to draw away.

'I can't,' Issy murmured. 'I shouldn't.'

He saw her eyes close against the radiance of the night sky, as though blocking out the world and surrendering to a fantasy she wished was real as he pulled her to his chest.

'Max,' she whispered, her voice a scratch that pierced the hardest part of him.

She wanted this he told himself, not stopping to ask himself what he was doing.

Her sinuous dress hugged every womanly curve, gliding over her breasts, inciting him to seek oblivion in the most primal way.

All of this was wrong. The impossible desire. The urgent throbbing in his sex. The swelling desire to command her mouth and kiss her again and again under the infinite sky. Until nothing but the two of them existed. Until the unhappiness of his childhood was submerged by a flood of other sensations. What did he have to lose? Nothing else helped him forget the pain of the past.

And then he remembered why the temptress

was there. She wasn't on the island to help him forget, but to force him to remember.

Max forced himself to pull away from her, steeling himself to the torrent of outraged words he knew would come from his cold rejection. Instead, she apologized, only adding to his guilt.

'I only meant to thank you,' she stammered, her voice a breathless whisper. 'It was my fault, I shouldn't have—'

'Shouldn't have thrown yourself at me?' he gritted out, his voice forged with steel. He sounded cruel but what else could he do? Her guilt only intensified his own.

'I'm a huggy sort of person. I'm not apologizing for that,' her eyes clashed with his, and all the breath rushed from his lungs.

'*Che cavolo*! You'd better leave me alone,' he growled, turning from her. 'Go back to New Zealand.'

'I can't.'

'Really, *mia tentatrice*?' he said, spinning around. She froze, wide-eyed like a doe, as he advanced toward her.

The sea pulsed with a rhythmic roar as he raked his fingers through the soft ripples of her hair, the silkiness of her tresses flooded his palms, flowing over his hands. He threaded his fingers around the back of her head and pulled her to him, plundering her mouth with a rough, demanding kiss.

Her lips were soft against his hard mouth, her taste sweet against his bitter sense of urgency. The quest to conquer her driven not just by lust but by a dangerous need to drive out the darkness. Like a black moth to an orb of light, he was drawn to her warmth as though being near to her might thaw the wall of ice inside him.

He took her mouth greedily selfishly, hungrily, spurred by a passion to possess her that was both liberating and frightening. For once he wasn't thinking. Not analyzing. Not controlling anything other than his desire to take her.

He could feel the way her heart quivered. He could sense the way her pulse fluttered in her neck. He could taste the breathlessness of her desire as he thrust his tongue in her mouth. Not breaking for air he commanded her mouth in his and inched her back along the torch-lined path toward her bure.

Pressing Issy against the door, he slid the straps of her dress from her shoulders. Madness engulfed him as the dress slithered to the ground. The glow of the firelight bathed Issy's skin in gold as if she'd been lit from within by molten amber.

'No, Max,' she murmured, her voice barely audible. But there was no denying he hadn't felt her desire as his hands cupped her breasts, feeling the tiny torturous mound of her hardened nipples responding to his touch. 'Oh, God,' she sighed, folding into him.

Everything felt inevitable as he lifted her in his arms. He was taking things too fast, spiraling out of control but he no longer cared.

They were two consenting adults. Male and female. Opposites in every way but in this one act, they were together. United by desire, but alone. No one would ever know.

A sexual need so urgent and shocking engulfed him in waves of need so powerful that it drowned out every rational emotion, flooding the chasm of need, filling the unrelenting void.

Her sweet musky scent breathed arousal as she lay in his arms, the supple softness of her bare skin against his body drove him wild. He kicked the door to the bure open and laid her on the bed.

Tugging his shirt over his head, he unbuttoned his pants, noticing her wide eyes riveted to him, hearing a tiny gasp as her eyes fell upon his manhood.

He wrenched his trousers down his legs and tore them from his feet. Clasping her ankles he slid her gently toward the edge of the bed.

Standing over her, he spread her legs. With probing urgent fingers, he pushed aside her panties and felt for her womanhood, smiling with satisfaction as he felt the hot river of her desire. Aware of nothing but the sexual oblivion, the sheer pleasure of release, he penetrated her, his body emptying of everything he knew.

Except her.

Standing naked before her, his need assuaged, reality returned in a cold blast of self-disgust and realization. She had not run. She had not fled. She had driven him to the edge with sweet temptation. What driving madness had possessed him?

Selfish, uncaring bastard. Losing control would come at a cost. The only unknown was what price would she extract?

18

———————

'Hit me with another,' Max set the crystal tumbler down onto the granite bar harder than he should. The bartender turned at the sound and glanced back at his supervisor. The older Fijian nodded slowly, his eyes signaling his understanding, as though sensing the conflict stabbing Max's heart. No doubt they'd both seen their share of normally sober guests at Max's resort drowning their conflicting emotions in a heady mix of alcohol.

Fire and ice, Max mused clenching the tumbler as he stared at the rocks of ice submerged like the Titanic below the burnt orange hue of the whiskey. Like a nymph from a Waterhouse painting, Issy's face shimmered on the surface of the amber liquid —ethereal, desirous, seductive.

If he wasn't such a rational man he'd think she

had cast a spell over him. Why else would a plain Jane make him so reckless? Yet she wasn't plain. Not in the way ordinary girls were. There was something unique about Issy and it was driving him crazy.

Either that, he decided, or the surgeons that had operated on him meddled with a vital valve in his heart—joining it up with a circuit of feeling he would prefer remained defunct.

'*Quei bastardi.* You sad, sorry fuck,' he cursed, pushing the glass aside unwilling to block out what he knew he must face. He had acted irrationally and irresponsibly, dressing her like a siren and driving her to him, only to find he couldn't stand the heat. Drinking wouldn't obliterate his guilt. He'd already lost control once. It was a mistake he didn't plan to repeat.

Anger slapped inside his stomach as the sky rumbled with the threat of rain. Two sets of parents had repeatedly taught him how easily vows could be broken. "You're just like your father," his mother threw at him every time she was displeased. Her relentless attacks were like one giant affirmation. But maybe she was right. He was just like his father.

A heartless philanderer.

Wasn't that the reason he threw himself into his work? It certainly beat having his creative energies devoured by a loveless marriage. What was it Leonardo da Vinci had once said, he wondered, staring into the black void of the stormy sky. "Marriage is like putting your hand into a bag of snakes in the hope of pulling out an eel."

Max's thoughts coiled around the first time he laid eyes on the enchantress. The memory of Issy standing by the water's edge, wide-eyed and enraptured when he'd gone to the sea snake's rescue made his loins throb with dangerous need. Need that rapidly accelerated when his thoughts slithered toward the enraptured passion they'd shared. The memory of Issy's scent of arousal, the sinuous silky feel of her soft tousled hair burying into his chest, the flaming heat of her breath, hot and elicit against his neck as he took her again, and again, bit through his thoughts.

He would have to atone for his sins, he would have to face his demons, he would have to confront his past. Someday. But not today. Nor tomorrow. Nor any of the four days he was stuck on this wretched Pacific atoll with a woman that made his passions flare.

Passion.

That dangerously, disastrous flame-coloured word. Passion—uncontrollable, untameable emotion which like a poison, unless he took care, would have no antidote, binding her to him for eternal hell. What the hell had he been thinking?

That was just the problem he wasn't thinking.

Max stared into the void of the bruised and moody sky. His darker side had won, the side that retreated from the light into an insatiable quest for lust and seduction. The side that like Adam tempting Eve to mortal sin had thrown Issy an apple then fled from her bed, abdicating responsibility. He had corrupted her. Then he had run.

But why? He raked his fingers through his hair, then gripped his head in his hands. He had spent his life moving from conquest to conquest. He had never cared that his sexual affairs were devoid of feeling? He had preferred it that way.

And why couldn't he shake the sense that Issy would no more bite his head off than she would impede his success? Why despite everything his rational mind stormed and shouted, did he feel with such clarity that she had come to his rescue?

Reaching for his iPhone Max swiped the screen with an impatient flourish. He couldn't block out the annoying woman who was creating mayhem with his emotions, but he could absorb himself in his work. He scrolled through the hundreds of emails clogging his inbox since he'd last logged on. A pang of pride coursed through his torso as he registered the responses Sophia had copied him into.

He forced his mind from Issy and focused on the formidable job Sophia was doing when, as if she'd read his thoughts, a text message illuminated his screen.

"r u playing nicely?"

Max pressed his lips into a grim line. It was as though his sister had sixth sense, but then didn't all women.

No, he hadn't played nicely. Not at all. He wouldn't lie. Pressing his thumb firmly on the off button he watched the screen flicker and then die, noticing with surprise how liberating it felt to hand over the reins and disconnect from the world of unrelenting responsibilities.

From the flurry of replies, Sophia was not only excelling but also thriving. Max gave a wry smile. Why hadn't he ceded control to her earlier? A whoosh of air escaped from his lungs, relaxing the normally granite-hard tightness in his chest as it did so.

He lifted his head and gazed around his estate. Sophia was right. What was it all for? What would be his legacy? Who would remember him when he was gone? Who would love him when he was alive? Was closing himself off as he had all these years living his best life?

Max pulled out a sketchbook and picked up his pen. The blank page glared at him. Taunting him with its infinite possibilities. Usually, he rose to the challenge, but as his pen hovered over the page nothing came.

Perhaps Issy was right. How could he create when he felt no joy? Felt no love? He was surrounded by beauty but felt nothing. Life to her seemed like a paint box of color. He envied her spontaneity, her curiosity, and fascination with her surroundings. She was everything he no longer was.

With her sunny optimism, her blind faith in humanity, her misplaced belief in the power of the heart, she was a painful reminder that for some life is lived with color and joy, spontaneity and surprise —not a gray wasteland of endless work demands, neutrality, control and predictability. Where Issy saw a rainbow, Max only saw unrelenting rain.

Issy, he reluctantly conceded was a painfully sharp reminder of all that he had lost. Maybe his sister and Issy were right. How could he move forward if he wouldn't face the past?

A bolt of lightning illuminated the sky. The raw, ragged crack exploded in the air, as it struck a coconut tree beyond the bar splitting it open. At the same time, something in his own consciousness ripped apart, as though the effort of sustaining the facade of a workaholic egomaniac had caught up with him. His chest surged and swelled.

For the first time in his life, he felt something.

For the first time in his life, he had touched someone who felt real.

Real.

Issy was so refreshingly real. Those great transparent, guileless eyes, vibrantly green like the rare sapphires he imported from Madagascar, as scarce as they were valuable. Priceless. To his surprise he found himself smiling as he recalled all the ways she tried to camouflage her true essence.

The pink, crazy hair. The chaotic blaze of colors she wore. The *"I don't-care-what-people-think-attitude."* But she did care, just as he cared. And he saw her just as she saw him. And it frightened him.

She had surrendered to him hoping like all women, that his kiss held a promise he was incapable of keeping. A heady rumble cracked the sky as if the natural world was expressing its frustration, tearing its hair out in a giant roar, shouting, "What are you running from?"

He didn't know. All he knew was he'd promised her nothing. Pledged nothing. Committed nothing. But even the knowledge that only his work possessed his heart did nothing to drown his nagging disquiet. Max felt the ache in his temples, the pressure in his head and the force coursing through his body as he fought to suppress the truth.

She had got to him.

She had made him feel.

19

Max suddenly felt light-headed and breathless. A surge of adrenaline lapped his body. It was back! His inspiration was back! He pushed back from the bar and shot to his feet. He needed to channel it. Now. Before it disappeared.

He said goodnight to his staff and headed along the torch-lit path to his clifftop studio. He felt like his limbs were filled with nitrous oxide, like he could walk on the ocean and bench-press two airliners.

Perhaps this woman who'd exploded into his world had entered his life for a reason.

There was no time to waste. He couldn't remember ever feeling so inspired. So certain. So liberated from constraint. What did every woman want? They wanted the confidence to be themselves. They wanted adventure. They wanted passion. They wanted color—not a gray wasteland of neutrality.

They wanted what Issy oozed so effortlessly.

He rushed into his studio and stood at his drawing board on the terrace overlooking the lagoon, glancing momentarily at the crashing waves below. How ironic that the woman inspiring his creativity didn't even know what she had. He swept his hands across the page in a drawing frenzy, abandoning all precision, all caution, all correctness— just as Issy did.

Tearing sheets of paper off as he filled them with designs, he laughed. Instead of feeling tense, he found himself smiling as he flourished his pen across the page.

Where once his designs had been inspired by inanimate architecture, ruled by precision and structure and rhythm—now they were inspired by the soul of a woman. He roughly sketched in uncharacteristically crazy lines. Fast. Furious—dare he admit it, fun? Each rapidly etched stroke more frenzied than the previous.

A vivid image of Issy's body, draped in his arms, gold shimmers sparkling across her voluptuous body, her creamy skin warmed by the moonlight rose from the page, encircling his imagination.

He was in no doubt she was sent as a test. A test

just like a recovering alcoholic on a deserted island who was given two precarious options—sip from her natural juices or suckle Satan's alcoholic elixir. Yes, he sighed feeling suddenly clear sighted. She was his passion test, just as Eve was to Adam.

His challenge was not to exploit, nor to succumb, nor would he treat her with disproportionate reverence. Whatever path their relationship took in the future, one thing was certain—he would channel everything into his work.

The knowledge was as disconcerting as it was liberating. Disconcerting because it meant letting go of everything he'd clung to. Liberating because perhaps he could finally free himself of the past and embrace the future. To survive he must adapt. If that meant experiencing all that Issy had to give, all she had to share, all that she offered, he would accept. She would be his muse.

The only question was would she agree to his terms?

20

———

Issy awoke to find herself alone in the huge bed, her body pulsing with heat. The first flames of the sun filtered in tangerine hues through the louvered doors, washing the room in an ethereal golden light. It was morning, a new day, a chance to start again and forget last night ever happened. But her body ached in ways that were foreign to her. She felt—

No! She closed her eyes, trying to suppress feelings she knew would only bring disappointment. Her blazing mind gave her no relief, burning instead with heated memories as she trailed her hand over the sheets where only a few hours ago she and Max had made love.

Amazing. She felt totally amazing. And along with those feelings, like a shadow crossing the sun, sauntered guilt. The night of passion that had been the most amazing sex she'd ever experienced should *never* have happened.

She rolled onto her back and looked up at the Modrani painting as her heart raced. Why had she let that happen? Was she just starved for affection, or was it because for the first time she felt a man really desired her?

A beam of sunlight spotlighted a tiny baby-blue bottle in the painting, standing between a transparent white vase, and an opaque black bottle. For some insane reason, it made her think of the beautiful children a union between her and Max could produce. Our son would be so handsome, she mused. His looks, her eyes. His dimples, her smile. His hair, their brains.

Issy's smile disappeared and her gut slopped with panic as reality loomed cold and glaringly bright.

God, what was she thinking?

That was the problem. Last night she hadn't reasoned about anything other than her fear of missing out on experiencing all that Max wanted to give. She hadn't anticipated the massive consequences of having sex.

Oh, God, she'd slept with her client.

The warm glow that had permeated every fiber

of her being when she'd woken disappeared and all that was left was freezing panic.

What had she done?

Last night had meant nothing to him. She wasn't dumb enough to pretend it had been personal. It wasn't about her. Seducing her, and then claiming her had been his way of pushing her away. He would know that she'd be left with no choice but to resign.

They were polar opposites, hardwired to always conflict. She was the hired help. He was the client. Whatever chemistry sparked between them last night hadn't changed that. The man didn't do emotion. She made a career of it. His heart and his head were disconnected by a sabre-sharp blade of logic. Her heart ruled her head—and her traitorous body, which despite all her attempts at reason, pulsed with need, tricking her into believing that someone who by all accounts was so wrong for her, was Mr. Perfect.

Dumb, dumb, dumb.

I'm being stupid, she censored herself. It's a childish crush, a dangerous infatuation made more palatable because he's strictly off-limits. Classic textbook stuff. Any psychoanalyst worth their fee would tell her that by falling for the hard-to-get-strictly-off-limits guy she was protecting herself from hurt. Essentially rejecting herself. Because when the inevitable rejection came she would have seen it coming first.

Falling for Massimilliano Balforni was like falling for a movie-star. Completely out of her league.

Issy's mouth twisted wryly. Perhaps Nancy was right, the reason she'd never found a love that lasted was because she always went for the wrong guy. Her training, her work and life experience heightened her knowledge of human behavior, and psychology—it just hadn't covered any module in love.

Paintings couldn't break your heart. Men did. Art, she reminded herself, swinging her legs out from the crumpled sheets and over the edge of the bed was her passion, her joy, her escape. Her love. She stood up, casting a brief look back at the bed. Mortification pulsed through her body as her gaze fell on the loved-stained sheets. She closed her eyes fruitlessly trying to blot out the blazing memory of their passionate encounter.

'And I certainly don't need a reminder of my mistake,' she said, tearing the sheets from the bed, and throwing them in a heap beside her feet. After James' betrayal, why would she even entertain the thought—no matter how great the fantasy—of a life with the ultimate heartbreaker.

Issy glanced momentarily up at the Morandi.

Art made her feel alive in a way that no man ever had

Until now.

Sex with Max had been unforgettable. And that was the problem. Somehow she had to delete him from her heart and erase him from her head.

The question was—how?

21

___

How could Max have flirted so outrageously with her? Issy ripped a large sheet of water-color paper from her pad. Thrusting firmly she pinned it to the board as she sat on the table on the deck outside her bure. Taking her widest brush she swept in liberal washes of water, then squeezed a blaze of scarlet red straight from the tube.

She'd done nothing wrong, she thought as she watched the paint bleed into the paper. She hadn't encouraged him at all. Issy splashed more water onto the paper, tipping the board slightly to stop the paint from dripping off the sides.

She hadn't led him on one little bit, she gritted flicking her brush rapidly and peppering the paper with spontaneous color.

He'd controlled the whole thing. Taken her to

the edge. Then pushed her over. And she'd let him. Was it desperation that stopped her resisting his advances? Or fear of missing out? Whatever it was she so shouldn't have gone there. But she would not be his victim. She would take back control, even if it meant quitting.

Pressing a tube of black paint to the page Issy etched a ragged outline of a man. That man. The infuriating man one who showed with the transparency of watercolor that he was toying with her. He had no heart. No feelings. No emotion. The only way she could rid herself of the painful memories he had triggered was to pour her emotions onto the paper.

Her heart raced as, guided only by her intuition, she squeezed a generous dollop of permanent rose onto the painting. She didn't stop to analyze why, of all the colors in her paint box, she'd been drawn to rose. Rose, the eternal symbol of romantic love.

Nor did she consider holding back on using her most expensive pigment when money was so tight. It would be worth splurging if she could exorcise her treacherous feelings for Massimilliano Balforni from her heart.

And it would be worth it if she could figure out how she was going to face him and get things back on track professionally. 'About last night,' she rehearsed, pushing the paint across the page. 'Last night was a mistake,' she said, layering in a thick wounded streak.

Stupid Issy. Of course it was a mistake. Max must be regretting every minute of it. Absorbing the excess pigment pooling across the page with her rounded brush, she dabbed at the hole she'd left for his heart, and layered in a wash of moody gray.

Feeling empowered by the new direction the painting was taking, Issy flounced her quill into a small pot of Indian ink. She roughly outlined large hands and fingers wrapped around a giant brush. In spite of everything that had happened, she began to enjoy herself.

'Now you'll have to play with my paints!' she said, stepping back from the painting and smiling. Taking some salt from a small container in her paint box she sprinkled it over the damp painting, smiling as the salt worked its magic, chasing away some of the pigment to make a lighter area beneath it. She loved the way she couldn't predict what was going to happen —that was half the fun.

Why was it, she worried, that she couldn't bring this same carefree abandon when she fronted up to Max and told him she was resigning? Why was she so preoccupied with how he was going to react? She needed to manifest more courage.

Put yourself on the page. Her Interactive Drawing Therapy training was so ingrained that the command came instinctively. Before she could put the brakes on, her subconscious did the bidding, unleashing repressed desires. She painted herself beside Max twirling like an elegant ballerina. on a pedestal, pausing mid-pirouette so Max could admire her.

Issy chuckled to herself. What fantasy. What nonsense. What make-believe. A man like Max who could have any woman would never admire her. And, being such an unfeeling brute he would most definitely never pause long enough to discover, let alone admire, who she really was.

She stood back and let the painting speak to her. Amidst the blaze of abstract color, she could just make out the outline of a flamenco dress. She seized the inspiration. A ballerina was far too tame.

She layered in a shot of illicit rouge to give the dress more boldness, twisting and rolling her brush to create giant ruffles like the hibiscus flowers perfuming Max's tropical paradise. She painted an arm swept across her breasts and the other whipped into the air with a defiant flourish.

The result was as eye-popping as it was dangerous. Just looking at the painting made her feel confident, full of passion and courageous fire. She felt like she could transcend the beliefs her mother's cruel taunts had imprinted so savagely. She felt like she could liberate herself from the ingrained feelings that she wasn't worthy.

She swept her brush into the pigment, then painted in a large scarlet flower tucked behind her ear. For one delicious, reckless moment she felt, like a bee to nectar, she was alluring enough to attract Italy's most eligible billionaire.

She placed the end of her brush in her mouth and chewed, twirling the ends of her own fuchsia pink hair as she studied the painting.

Put some feelings on the page, the voice commanded again, invoking another key mantra of her training. Grabbing a pastel from a box in her satchel she scribbled "Joyful. Sensual. Sexy. Loved".

Loved.

God, where did that come from? She'd never been loved. Not unconditionally. Not for who she truly was. She was only loved for who people wanted her to be. And even then whatever it was that drew men to her, it certainly wasn't love. Not everlasting love, anyway. What the hell did she know about love? And why would a man like Max love a girl like her when he could have any woman he desired?

She washed in some warm cobalt blue to cool things down, then chided herself for being so negative. Whatever had happened to her in the past she must never lose her optimism. She would never be like her mother bitter and complaining. 'It sucks that you've been hurt. But get over it,' she told herself, adding a splash of sunny yellow around her flamenco dancer. 'Dance like you've never been horribly hurt. Sing like you've never been seriously sad. Make love like—'

Issy sucked in air as her mind flashed back to Max. The way he took command of her lips, and the scorching feel of his skin beneath her fingers as she wrapped her arms around him. She felt her body stiffen and tremble as she folded into the memory. She stared blindly down at the trace of watercolor beneath her fingernails, hot tears clogging her eyes as she faced the unpalatable truth.

Max was everything she wanted—and feared, sexy, arrogant and emotionally frozen. Immersed in the world of painting Issy might be a dreamer but in all things Max she was a realist. She could paint her fantasies, recreate her dull life in visual splendor with symphonies of movement, color, and sound. But that was as 'real' as anything was going to get.

She tidied up her makeshift studio on the deck, leaving the saturated painting to dry, and padded to the bathroom to wash the nonsense out of her brushes, and remove all traces of their fated liaison under the shower. It was time to scrub up and prepare to resume the charade she had to play. Detached, consummate, *resigning*, professional.

She didn't need a man, she affirmed, ignoring the heaviness in her gut calling her a liar. She looked back at the woman in the painting as she stepped towards the bathroom.

Why did she look so bloody happy?

Their first art-therapy session was scheduled to begin in less than 30 minutes. Even though Issy doubted Max would show, it was important she was on time. She would tell him of her decision then.

She rattled through the bathroom vanity. 'Blast, no hairdryer.' She went to the phone beside her bed and dialed Tukana, the resort manager, and asked for one to be brought to the bure.

She jumped in the shower and placed a liberal dollop of Balforni shampoo in her palm, transforming her hair into a foaming prism of Frangipani bubbles when there was a firm knock on the door.

'Just a minute,' she shouted out. Turning off the water she stepped out of the shower, wrapped a towel around her, and scuttled to the door. 'Gosh that was quick,' she said, flinging it open.

'Oh crap!' She clenched the tiny piece of toweling tightly around her breasts as Max flashed her a wide-eyed glance and strode into the bure.

'Very Marge Simpson,' he said, gesturing to the foaming beehive on her head.

Issy lifted her right hand and patted her hair flat. A whisper of foam bubbled between them, then drifted through the open door, fluttering toward the azure sea.

'What are you doing here?' she asserted.

Max cast his eyes around the room, his gaze rested briefly on the sheets strewn on the floor then darted away. He was very adept at avoiding things, she thought, as she watched him scan the bure restlessly. He was also very adept at making her uneasy. Unless she was wrong, he did both on purpose.

But what she couldn't work out was what he was searching for. She followed his stare as his eyes narrowed warily. Then, with mortifying clarity, it dawned on her.

The painting!

22

The caricatured, frenzied portrayal of him. Complete with the tiny 'spray on' trunks he'd been wearing when they first met. There could be no mistaking the painting was of Max.

Forgetting she was virtually naked, the tiny bit of toweling barely covering her butt she flew across the room. Max caught up to her in three easy strides, his long legs chewing up the ground much faster than her five foot six inches would allow her to move.

Gripping the towel she reached out to grab the portrait. His hand closed firmly over hers. She felt her body stiffen and tremble. She could have nudged his hand away. She could have wrestled the painting from him. Instead, she stood still, enjoying the sensation she knew she would never experience again.

His gaze zeroed in on the hole she'd left for his heart. 'Very expressive,' he said, his tone grave.

Her brows drew together as she braced herself for a torrent of criticism. She was too mortified to care about the foam crawling down her neck and pooling along the swell of her breasts. She looked him in the eyes as she always did when she was criticized by her mother, and standing stiff like a soldier waiting for him to laugh at her stupid painting.

He smiled with a strangely gentle charm that shouldn't have complimented his eyes yet did. 'You've got real talent, *Principessa*. This is extraorindary. *Perfecto!*'

A surge of unexpected warmth scuttled through her. Was he seriously flattering her? *Again*? It would be easier to hate him if he had made a scene, told her that her painting was childish, the work of an amateur. Told her *she* was an amateur. But he said none of that.

Heat flared between them.

Issy drew back. Her legs shook, her knees felt weak, shaken by the ferocity of the desire she felt to kiss him, and the urgent desire to confide that she had never shared her paintings with anyone, fearing they would only confirm what she feared—that they were no good. That she was no good.

For all her degrees, and professional accomplishments and cultivated facade of togetherness she had a firm fear of rejection she'd never been able to shake. She was, after all, the skilled "I've-got-it-all-together-therapist" helping people with their problems, not facing her own vulnerabilities.

Her job as an art-therapist gave her identity, social validation, prestige, respect—and a steady paycheque that put a tiny roof over her bedsit. Who would she be if she was a starving artist? How would she pay the bills? She was already struggling as it was.

If she had more guts, more courage, more-self-belief perhaps she might have tried harder. Sent the paintings abandoned under her bed to galleries and entered competitions. But then—shaking her head, she didn't believe she had it in her to be a great artist.

'It's nothing. Just a scribble,' she said, staring at her feet.

'I've clearly under-estimated you,' he said against the lush seduction of his mouth. 'In fact, I know very little about you. I don't know why you've run away for Christmas, why you're hiding your real talent, or what you plan to teach me. I know next to nothing about you,' he said moving way to close.

'Although I do know,' he said, his voice dangerously low, 'That you have a violet butterfly tattooed at the base of your neck.'

Painting on her most unaffected smile she spoke with saccharine politeness, 'I'm glad you noticed it.' She backed toward the door and held it open. 'Now if you'll excuse me I really do have to get dressed.'

His eyes ran the length of the braided edge of the towel stretched tightly across her generous chest then traveled with leisurely thoroughness down her body resting for a long uneasy moment where the towel finished at the top of her thigh.

'Please,' she said, loathing the fact that her mind wanted nothing more right now than to be a million miles away from him but her body was screaming, 'Take me.' She should run before she was pushed, and stop thinking about a one-off fling that was never going to happen again.

Oh God this was horrible.

She cleared her throat and mentally rehearsed the script she'd been practicing all day. But she'd been dressed then, and now she was standing virtu-ally naked in front of the man who had intimate knowledge of every part of her body.

Mortification didn't cut it. Shame-faced humilia-tion did. She took a deep breath. The quicker she got it out, the quicker he could do what he always intended and bundle her out.

She glanced out the open door, noting with an

unexpected pang of disappointment Tukana waiting beside the Land Rover below. The engine was running. No doubt the plane was already fired up to go, too. God, he couldn't wait to get rid of her. Well, she couldn't wait to go. And she would tell him first.

Suddenly she was angry with him. And she was angry with herself. It was embarrassingly unclassy to have a morning-after encounter, especially when she was half-naked and he appeared so nonplussed.

'You don't have to run me off the island. I'm leaving anyway.' She said, hoping he didn't notice her voice quiver.

'Leaving?' his expression revealed nothing of his thoughts.

There was no "It's not your fault," to take the sting out of rejecting her. No fake romantic words —"you're a lovely girl. I'm sure you'll meet a lovely man one day."

None of that. De Nada. And he wasn't about to offer up some false hope of happily ever after. He wasn't about to give her anything except a flippant compliment about her childish painting that she doubted he even meant.

She'd been right. What happened last night meant nothing. Perhaps she should be grateful. Perhaps she could learn a lot from such a consummate master of cold selfish, indifferent detachment. She could mirror the same indifference. Well, if he wasn't going to mention the pink elephant in the room she bloody well would.

'Last night was a mistake. One that I intend paying for,' her voice was rougher than she intended and instead of being non-plussed Max looked at her as though she was quite mad.

'I'm leaving—on your jet plane. Here's my bill for the time I've spent already and my letter of resignation,' she said handing both to him. She'd earned her money and then some, brushing aside a tiny voice telling her she had a nerve asking him for a dime.

He arched an eyebrow. His eyes widened. His lips pressed into a firm line as he looked at her, making no effort to take what she held in her hand.

The pages dangled limply as she kept her arm outstretched.

The only thing breaking the awkward silence was the whirring of the wooden fan above their heads, and the shrill chorus of birds flying through the humid morning air.

She anchored her feet to the tiled floor, digging in her resolve. Her arm throbbed, aching with the effort of keeping it straight.

Still, he did not move. He did not speak. He did not cede.

Finally his command splintered the silence.

'No!' His voice was raw and ragged, not controlled and measured like it normally was, which threw her.

'I'm sorry, my mind's made up,' she said, making a Herculean effort to keep her voice steady.

'I do the firing,' he said, his tone made it clear that in this matter all things were non-negotiable.

Anger licked at her throat, flaming a rage she fought to suppress. A rage she wished for one reckless minute she could give voice to, but she never did. Never had. Never would. Growing up in a house filled with anger and shouting, hiding under the bed, forcing her fingers in her ears, she'd vowed she would never inflict that kind of torture on another. No matter how well deserved.

Boy, would she like to yell back, and wipe that control right off his face. Instead, she smiled, as she always did, and imagined a soft, spongy bubble in sparkly pink surrounding her. The kind that was infused with violet and yellow and all the colors of the rainbow when the sunlight caught it.

She imagined herself far away, as she had as a child, far away from disagreement and unpleasantness. But instead of feeling happy all she saw was her horrid little bedsit and the flashing light on her phone telling her that her mother and her toad of an ex were expecting her for Christmas.

23

'I didn't take you for a quitter,' Max said in the voice he only ever had to use once with his staff, never twice. Her eyes flashed as he hoped they would.

'I'm not a quitter,' she said, with a fierceness that surprised him. It was fighting talk, which he admired, but her warrior words only sat on the surface of her delectable face. Beneath the bravado she looked as vulnerable as if he had just ordered her to drop her towel and parade in front of him stark naked.

But she had already done that. And for that he felt terrible. He would never subject her to that indignity again. He wouldn't tell her that. But he'd expected her to fight to stay, to cling to false hope—not to run away.

Once again she'd surprised him. But there was something else, something, a vulnerability he'd seen once before, which made him feel surprisingly protective. He wanted to wrap her in a soft robe.

Her fingers gripped the edge of the toweling, her knuckles white. 'I don't leave people, they leave me,' she said softly. Then as though thinking she'd said too much she added, 'But in this case my professionalism requires I leave you. Everything would just be awkward if I stayed.'

'No,' Max thundered. 'I can't allow you to leave.' He needed her. But he couldn't tell her that. He wouldn't tell her that. He had never needed anyone before. Self-reliance had kept him safe.

'I'm sorry? You can't allow me to leave? Are you forcing me to stay?'

'And if I were? Would that be so bad?'

She gazed toward the airfield as though wondering how she would get off the island, then turned toward him looking directly at him as though trying to fathom what was going on in his mind. Good luck trying, he had no idea himself. He just knew he needed her.

'I won't, I can't—let you go. You have something.' *Something I need.*'

'What? What could I possibly have that with all your wealth, all your connections, all the choices that your money can buy, you can't import from somewhere else?'

You. It's you. There's something about you, he wanted to say but didn't. He didn't know what it was about her or why she and no other woman had made him feel the way he did. All he knew was that for the first time in far too long his creativity was back. And there was no way he was going to let her know that she could take credit for that. Not without her realizing she had some power over him.

'I can recommend someone else...' she said in that innocent voice of hers that was etched into his soul, as much a part of him as his own.

'I need *you*,' he thundered at the rawest level.

Her gaze touched his, then moved away as she turned from him, 'I'm sorry—I can't. It's better if I go.'

The woman was impossible. Did he really have to beg?

~

'Chiedo scusa. I'm sorry.'

Sorry. Words she'd *never* heard from any man. His brutal apology was as surprising as the hammering in her chest.

'No, I'm sorry,' she said. 'I crossed the line. It was my fault.'

'Do you always apologize when it's others that should take the blame?'

Yes. She always played peacekeeper, she always tried to make others feel better. Growing up everything was always her fault.

'It was unprofessional of me. You didn't know what you were doing. Stress makes people do things out of character—'

He gave a humorous laugh, '*Isabella,* I knew exactly what I was doing. Escaping. Taking ruthless advantage of a kind, caring young woman who ordinarily wouldn't have found herself anywhere near a man as damaged as me. And it wasn't out of character. I've been pulling that stunt most of my life. Pushing people away. But I don't want to push you away.'

'You don't?' she stammered.

'I used you. For that, I apologize. But something happened last night. I don't know—' He drew a deep breath as though wrestling with what he wanted to say and what he felt he should say. 'It's just that for the first time I felt inspired. Not at first,' he corrected. 'At first, I felt rotten for pouncing on you like that. I shouldn't have done it. I was being selfish.'

Issy's heart skipped. *It was progress.* As much as she would have liked to blurt out that she enjoyed every minute of being pounced on she kept her trap shut. Finally, he was opening up to her. A tiny hairline crack, but a glimmer of light, nevertheless.

'I'd like to make it up to you. If you're still determined to go, I can't stop you. But at least let me show you the real Fiji.' His voice was much too hoarse and he saw that she sensed it. 'Bring your paints.'

24

'You're missing everything, Max,' Issy said through wind-blown hair that caught in her mouth as she spoke. She stuck her head out of the Land Rover as they sped past authentic Fijian villages devoid of the trappings of western life.

Potted dirt roads led to homes whose walls formed a tapestry of natural woven panels, wooden planks and corrugated iron painted in peony pink and banana yellow. Outhouses billowed smoke as daily meals were cooked over open fires while chickens roamed and children played.

'Look!' Issy cried, pointing towards two plump birds. 'Oh my God, aren't they beautiful.'

'Ah, these are Flame Doves, also known as the Orange Fruit Dove,' said Tukana, gripping the steering wheel with one hand, his other pointing to the trees where the birds were nesting.

'They're so cute. They have rock-melon orange feathers and lime feather heads—as though they really are what they eat,' Issy giggled.

Max felt his heart tug. It was extraordinary how much pleasure this woman got out of life. Her exuberant spirit was infectious and he found himself relaxing.

'They take a long time to find a mate, but once united they never part,' Tukana said, winking at Kerela, his wife, who was riding up front beside him.

'Oh, that's so adorable.' The delectable freckles sprinkled over the bridge of Issy's nose like hundreds and thousands on fairy bread crinkled as she grinned. God, he'd like to eat her.

He already knew she tasted delicious. Max took a deep breath and thrust his head out of the window inhaling giant gulps of fragrant air. But the spellbindingly seductive scent of frangipani and hibiscus affected him, like an aphrodisiac.

Increasing his sexual desire was not what he needed at all. What he needed was a freezing cold shower. Max dredged illicit thoughts of her from his mind and fixed his gaze firmly out the window. It was not the gray humorless jungle of towering formidable high-rises of his New York offices, nor the analytical, linear, meticulously ordered grid of Milan's streets. Nor was it the frantic scramble of fashion week, everyone fighting to conquer each other. It was a golden Eden, an organic and unstructured melody of shapes and colors which blended effortlessly together.

Just like Issy, he mused, dizzied by the chaotic blaze of tropical fruit trailing in a riot of blistering yellows and over-ripe oranges across her shapeless ankle length kaftan. There was something hopelessly enchanting about her. He found himself wondering whether the blaze of creativity that had infused his dreams after they'd first slept together would accelerate if they slept together again.

It would be fun trying were it not for the lingering feelings for her that deepened as they spent more time together, feelings that were as foreign to him as they were addictively unnerving.

No doubt about it, he was in trouble. He pondered his situation while gazing at the ominous clouds quickly building up across the sky.

25

A chorus of cries, accompanied by a wave of giggling and a sea of flailing arms and skinny legs, followed the Land Rover as it rattled down the lumpy dirt road, driving deeper and deeper into virgin rainforest. Children with huge glistening brown eyes ran alongside them as they approached the village.

'Bula!' a large man shouted at the top of his lungs, grinning as he emerged from a simple thatched building. Women glanced up from their weaving, waving and laughing as Max got out of the car and went to the boot.

'Toys and things for school,' he said, pulling out exercise books, pens, and pencils and passing them to the Fijians. 'And gifts too. For Christmas.'

Issy looked at him, unable to stop herself from smiling.

'It's difficult to get books in the islands,' Max said, thrusting his hands in his pockets.

'That's very generous,' she said, looking at the sack overflowing with goodies, respect deepening. James had hated children. And he was stingy. Even though he had buckets of money he never gave anyone anything. His was a Scrooge's Christmas.

But Max was a modern day Santa Claus, she thought, smiling as the children swarmed around him. Pride, or something surprisingly comfortable, swelled her heart. She was seeing a different side of him and it felt dangerously good. He was dressed in leather loafers, cotton loose-fitting trousers, which fit snugly over his firm to-die-for butt. And a black polo shirt that clung to his steel-honed chest, ridged and muscled in ways that defied belief—that made her mouth water and her knees feel shaky. He was gorgeous. He was something far more intoxicating than merely gorgeous, more overwhelming than simply handsome, and yet he was a complicated melody of thoughtfulness and powerful male abstraction besides.

Jolted back to awareness she realized he was looking at her. And it took every bit of self-preservation not to let out the high-pitched sound that clamored for release in her throat. Mirrored glasses hid his eyes but it was as if he was looking right into her soul. Her chest fluttered—in his shades she saw her future. Or dreamed she did, she told herself, climbing out of the jeep. She needed air—lots of it. She needed to shake her traitorous feelings from filling her head with silly nonsense, unattainable fantasies.

Gripping the fan she'd fashioned out of paper, she fluttered it in front of her face. He was Mr. Cool and Detached—where she was Ms. Hot and Totally Enamored, she mused wiping beads of perspiration from her brow.

He was getting to her in a way she knew would only end disastrously. She was Plain Chalk and he was Mr. Unattainable, she reminded herself as she lifted her camera from around her neck and fixed the lens on the children. Keep busy, she told herself, focus on everyone but him.

'Beautiful,' cried one of the children.

'Handsome man,' giggled several of the older women.

Issy smiled at the children encircling him as he handed out gifts. She envied the way the Fijians just said what they felt about him. No inhibition. No pretense. He was a terrifically good-looking man. If she wasn't working for him and wasn't so afraid of his rejection, she would cry out to him too. "Handsome, sexy, thoroughly irresistible man."

Instead, she hovered in the background taking photos, pretending not to be interested in him one little bit.

The village sat on the fringe of the coast. On the hill above them sat a simple white church, with a large white wooden cross, overlooking the village. Even though the cross itself had nothing to do with Christmas itself, it was for some reason, it was a comforting reminder of what Christmas was really meant to celebrate—a tradition that many people had forgotten.

She took a few photos of the building and the surrounding landscape and turned her attention back to the children gathering around Max. She felt her heart tug as she watched the man she'd only ever seen as remote and aloof suddenly spring to life. Taking a rugby ball from the sack of toys he ran through the village kicking it ahead of the clutch of giggling children who followed him as though he was the Pied Piper.

Issy put the camera into Shutter Priority mode, choosing a fast shutter speed, and captured him having fun. No matter how important he believed his job was, looking at the photos would remind him that there was more to life than adoring fans and wealth. For the first time since they'd met he looked relaxed and happy.

She watched him through the lens. That beautiful, impossibly strong body could definitely not have been the product of a squad of personal trainers, and surely he would never squander time away from work toiling on modern gym equipment. He employed every part of his extreme physicality in everything he did. He was a sleek, powerful machine.

Suddenly her feelings overwhelmed her, pummeling her from all angles. Her past and the present twisted together into a tense knot that she couldn't begin to unravel, — and was afraid to prod lest she fall apart and show him too much. She lifted the camera from her face, glancing at Max as she turned to walk away.

She watched as one of the older boys tackled him, wrapping taut muscular arms around his ankles. Max fell to the dirt. She braced herself for a torrent of rage, imagining he'd be angry that his beautiful clothes were soiled. But there was no sound. No movement. No sign of life.

She held her breath as he lay unmoving on the dusty earth. The boys held their breath too. They leaned closer. And still he didn't move.

Fear knotted her gut.

She was about to run to him when he let out a roar like a lion, and then laughed as he reached up with one perfectly chiseled arm and pulled the boys to the ground.

Laughing, Issy clicked off a line of photos, following his movement as he rolled in the dirt gripping the ball tightly, refusing to cede it to the growing group of boys descending upon him. Then with an incredible display of strength he soared to his feet. The boys sprung away, in awe of his power. With formidable agility, clutching the ball to his side, he ran toward the goal posts at the far end of the field, near at the edge of the village.

A little girl who Issy guessed was about four-years-old, with a spray of curls and dark chocolate eyes, tugged at her skirt tearing her attention away. The little girl pointed at the camera. Issy knelt down and showed her the photos she had taken. The girl nestled in her lap and was quickly joined by several other children.

'Funny man,' Issy said, her pulse fluttering as she swiped through the screen with her finger, sliding through the photos. 'Silly,' she giggled. Pinching the image with her fingers she zoomed closer, savoring for one delicious moment the tempered steel of his marvelous body.

'I'm glad you find me amusing.' The deep velvet voice held just a trace of humor and the sound sent quivers running through her skin.

Issy's face flamed. Sprung again. She fixed her eyes on his sleek loafers as his powerful frame cast a shadow over her. She lifted her head. Her eyes met

his and she was lost in a chorus of sensation too be-
wildering to understand. She felt his power sing
through her. The desire to be held in his arms almost overwhelmed her.

Dazed, Issy rose to her feet. Something hot and
dangerous burned between them.

'I need to take off my clothes.' His voice was so
muffled it almost disguised the cut of his words, the
way they cleaved into her, through her.

She watched as he retreated back to the Land
Rover to strip off his shirt wondering if he always
traveled on a day trip with a spare change of clothes.
She was so distracted she didn't notice Kerela approaching.

'Come on. Come and see how we make the
Masi,' Kerela said, sensing Issy's mind was
elsewhere.

'What is Masi?'

'Masi is the cloth of the Gods. Masi can make
magic.'

26

———————

'You're lucky,' Kerela said, glancing back toward Max.

Lucky? Issy followed Kerela's gaze, noticing her heart kick as Max tore off his shirt and placed it in the back of the Land Rover.

Was it luck that brought this excruciatingly handsome man to her side? Luck that maneuvered him with the stealth of a black panther into her bed? Luck that would take him away from her in less than four days?

She felt her heart muscles tense and then relax —the push-pull of desire and fear, the tensing of her shoulders as she fought the familiar fear of abandonment. Why the hell did she care?

'Without Mr. Balforni our culture would disappear,' Kerela said, as she led Issy toward the edge of the village. Chickens squawked and wild pigs grunted around their feet as a constant tap-tap-tap sound of something being pounded, rang through the village.

'What do you mean?' Something like respect tugged at Issy's heart as she walked beside her towards a large open-sided thatched hut.

'It was Mr. Balforni's idea to attract tourists like you here. We are just putting the finishing touches on our Fiji Eco Tour, a one-day unique Fiji tour where you experience our various natural, traditional and historical sites and activities that are of significance to the people of Fiji. You are our first couple.'

She should have reminded Kerela that they weren't a couple but realized with a start that she didn't want to. And she didn't want to detract from the excitement and pride Kerela obviously felt about what the villagers had achieved.

'This is one of a rapidly decreasing number of villages where tradition has escaped commercialism. The tourist trade has its benefits,' Kerela added, 'bringing much-needed money to the village and it allows our traditional arts to survive. But it's bad too because many traditional skills and crafts are being slowly diminished.

'It was Mr. Balforni who encouraged us to keep the traditional ways. In many of the other villages, their culture has been corrupted. Woodcarvings of turtles and spears for tourists are quickly churned out for the dollar. Quality decreases and the soul of Fiji is lost. But here in the village there are still people who know what they are doing.' Kerela flashed a wide-eyed look then dissolved into laughter. 'Nice Bula shirt!' she said giggling at Max rejoined them.

His left eyebrow grew into a slight peak at the center, giving him an expression of perpetual mischief, but his firm mouth held no trace of amusement. His sensual fingers ran over the vibrant blue shirt, trailing the bananas and lingering over the scattering of red hibiscus flowers.

'*Gracie mille.*' He offered a bemused smile. 'It was Isabella's idea that I embrace the spirit of Fiji. How do I look?'

'Like a tourist,' Kerela said, dissolving into laughter.

Issy felt her eyes tear. She would have wagered a bet she'd never get him into that gaudy shirt, let alone see him wear it in public. And she loved him for it. Wiping at her mouth, she covered her lips, biting them to hide a smile.

'Today the women are making traditional Masi mats to celebrate the wedding of the chief's daughter,' Kerela said. 'Mat-weaving is taught to nearly every village girl.'

Mothers with wise weather-worn faces sat cross-legged on woven mats beside their daughters and granddaughters. The older women had a beam of wood that looked like a long stool, stretched above their knees, as they pounded the thin fibrous bark with a worn wooden mullet.

'Making Masi is women's work. With powerful arms like yours you should go ad be useful to the men,' Kerela said to Max, gesturing toward a group of villagers wielding machetes. 'Go with Tukana, he will take you to the woodcarvers. They are leaving soon to collect more bark.'

To Issy's surprise, Max smiled with calm amusement and obeyed Kerela's command. She hadn't expected he'd be a hands-on, hunter-gatherer type. Not with those manicured hands. But, once he was away from his carefully cultivated estate it seemed everything about him was different, she mused, releasing an appreciative sigh.

'Don't work too hard, Isabella, ' Max's penetrating blue eyes combed Issy's face as he turned to her. 'Hard work can kill you.'

A strange and disturbing tug yanked on her heart, as though a vine like an umbilical cord connected them as she tore her gaze from him.

'This is from the paper mulberry tree,' Kerela said, picking up a flattened piece of bark the color of tea. 'Now it is like cloth and has many uses,' she said, passing it to Issy.

Issy felt a stab of longing as her fingers stroked the warm, fibrous fabric. She looked at the community of women before her and envied their closeness. She wasn't familiar with that kind of love. For a Nano-second the desire to be on the receiving end of it, from someone, anyone, even Max, was so powerful it made her heart ache.

What would it be like to have someone love you forever?

27

She and her mother had never experienced the closeness these women shared. And things only worsened over the years. While her behavior was understandable following her abandonment by Issy's father, Issy and she were always competing. At least her mother was.

The put-downs whenever Issy approached anything like success, the snide remarks, the lack of acknowledgment when she did well. The guilt her mother made her feel when she outshone her siblings. None of this existed here. Everyone shined, and everyone encouraged each other's gifts and the pursuit of excellence.

Growing up Issy quickly learned it was easier not to shine. But no matter what she attempted, or how she tried to appease others, she never felt accepted. She never felt she belonged. She never felt loved for who she really was.

A young mother swaddled her baby in a Masi cloth singing softly to it as she worked. As though sensing Issy's stare the baby turned toward her, swallowing Issy's heart in giant chocolate eyes.

'Masi is an ancient art—it contains the spirit of the land it comes from, the tree it was part of, and also contains the essence of the women who beat the cloth and decorate it. Masi can make magic. See this pattern?' Kerela said, picking up a piece of fiber and trailing her fingers along the intricate patterns. 'All the Masi contains a story, a story sacred to the women and their community. A story of dreams and longings and possibilities.'

Issy felt her fingers tremble as she took the fabric Kerela handed to her. She glanced back to the baby who still stared at her. Her heart pulsed. What was her story? What was her narrative? Would it end happily?

'Would you like to create your own Masi?' Kerela asked.

Issy nodded. She didn't wait to be asked twice.

The sound of the women singing as she sat amongst them infused her like a warm blanket around her soul. Her thoughts returned to that night she'd spent with Max. Had she not surrendered to him that night she'd never have known that in his arms she could experience the true meaning of rapture, the momentary feeling of safety, security, belonging.

She found herself wishing with pounding intensity that the story she might create for her Masi would be one that made an impossible dream come true. A warm breeze fluttered through the grass hut and she found her mind drifting. She imagined what it would feel like to wear her Masi on their wedding day, encircling them both in an unbreakable union.

As if! Picking up the mallet she joined in the rhythmic pounding, finding it profoundly therapeutic as the fibrous bark slowly changed into soft cloth.

Kerela directed a smile at Issy as though reading her thoughts. 'He's a keeper,' she murmured.

A keeper? As if! Issy increased her tempo, pounding the bark with added intensity. No man she'd loved had stayed. Love was fleeting. Clenching the mallet she pounded harder.

'We're just...' Just what? Friends? She hadn't known him long enough to be a friend. Yet they shared so many interests and he was kind to her. Lovers? Well, she could hardly confess to that.

She was ashamed to admit her breach of professionalism to anyone, especially not to this very devout Fijian woman where marriage and family were sacrosanct.

And she couldn't tell anyone that he was her client as she was sworn to secrecy. Instead, she sat in silence. A trickle of longing crawled on millipede legs through her chest as she surveyed the women. She envied the simplicity of their lives, the certainty the women and the young girls had. She gazed at the little girls with their wild puffs of curls seated opposite the most experienced senior weavers. They would marry a young boy from a local village and their families and culture would help them stay together. They loved each other. This was something Issy had never experienced in her own family.

'It is in God's hands,' Kerela said, gesturing to the wall opposite them. 'That is a God house, made from knotted coconut fiber—even though we believe in Jesus we honor the old ways. You can summon the Gods and ask them to tell your future. What will be, will be, no matter how you resist.'

Issy nodded politely. How could she tell Kerela that sometimes she felt that even God had abandoned her? How could she explain that no amount of petitioning could take away her growing sense of unease? Despair and longing iced through her. Was she destined to live her life on her own? A lonely spinster without her own family?

The women stopped singing briefly as a young

woman of around 19 appeared in the doorway, beside her stood a young man, carrying a little baby swaddled in a ceremonial Masi. They gazed at each other and the baby with such love it made Issy's heart melt.

'It's the chief's younger son and his wife,' Kerela said.

Issy's hands clamped tight over her heart as if she was afraid it might burst from her chest and shatter on the floor. This kind of familial love, this kind of loyalty, wasn't something she knew. Her mother had never forgiven Issy's Dad for leaving them. She'd never been able to love Issy, her first-born because her heart had been abandoned by a man who didn't care. Issy tried to love her mother, but she'd never given Issy a chance. Her Dad? Well, were it not for the random cards at Christmas you'd never think he existed.

'Do you have children, Issy?' Kerela asked.
'No.'
Turning, she said sweetly, 'Oh what a pity. But you are still young. There is still time,' she said kindly. 'But don't leave it too late. I will petition the gods and I will pray for you.'

Issy nodded slowly, suppressing desperate hope when she noticed Max standing in the doorway, observing the God house.

Fierce blue eyes met hers and Issy felt as if she

was being suffocated. She lifted her hand and loosened the scarf around her neck. Maybe it was his posture. Maybe it was the look in his eyes, but suddenly her heart was pounding.

'Did somebody die?' Tukana said, peering across his broad nose, as he studied them.

Issy shook her head. What must he be wondering? Max and she must look like they were in the middle of a funeral. Either that or they looked decidedly guilty.

'No, no. Not at all,' Issy said, quickly rising to her feet.

'Are you ready?' Kerela asked.

'Ready?'

'The Kava ceremony is an important aspect of visiting any village. But first, we need your help.'

Was she mistaken, or did something far too mischievous flame in Tukana's eyes?

28

'A honeymoon photo?' Issy jolted as if she'd been electrocuted. She spun to face Max, 'Is this another one of your little surprises? Another one of your ways to avoid doing some serious work?'

He shrugged and flung his arms wide, palms facing upwards as if to say he knew nothing, but it was not an unpalatable idea.

'The models haven't turned up,' the photographer explained. 'I've got to head back to the mainland tomorrow and the evening is so perfect.'

'I'm sorry. You'll have to find someone else,' Issy said, fixing Max with a gaze that she hoped would leave him in no doubt she was not gagging to kiss him. Turning her gaze down the virgin white beach fringed with coconut trees, she prayed that another couple would magically appear, but nope. De Nada.

The fates were conspiring against her. It was all going from bad to worse.

'The two of you are perfect,' the photographer insisted. 'So natural—and that shirt,' he said, gesturing to Max. 'What can I say? It captures the fun and joy that Fiji and its people offer. We want people to see the beauty of this village.'

Perfect? Perfect would be if anyone but her was in the photo. Perfect would be if she could to do a runner. Her first instinct was to continue to refuse but that would be churlish, while also drawing attention to her discomfort. And hadn't Kerela told her how important tourism was to the village. Besides she always found it hard to say no, and the photographer was obviously in a pickle.

'We'd be happy to help,' Max said, with a far too compliant smile, 'Wouldn't we, *mia cara*?'

'We would?' she stammered.

Max turned to where the photographer was setting up the tripod. 'How do you want us?'

'Romantic.'

Issy closed her eyes. Was this really happening? She took a deep breath willing the sea gods to swallow her now.

'Perhaps if you can hold hands, so I can get the angle right while I get set up,' he said, busying himself with the settings on his camera. An assistant held a gold foil reflector cloth toward the sun, then maneuvered it in slow movements until it illuminated them both is a wash of flattering light.

Issy felt her shoulders tense. Hands, it was only holding hands, she told herself, as she waited for Max to reach for her, telling herself desperately that it was like acting. It was all for the best. More tourism would bring much-needed money to the village, allowing better schools to be built for the children.

Willing her mind to remain calm was fine until Max laced his fingers through hers. Their palms met, and her pulse soared. Perspiration beaded on her chest. There is no chemistry. There is no chemistry, she chanted in her mind, praying the affirmation would override her pulsing body.

'Great. Come a little closer. Great. Now look into each other's eyes,' the photographer said, crouching as he looked through the viewfinder. 'I need more emotion. More passion. Imagine it's your honeymoon night. You're ravenous with desire.'

If she didn't know better she'd think the photographer was a set-up. He was clearly relishing his role, directing them as though he were Peter Jackson urging the cast on for an Oscar winning performance.

Max didn't look like he needed any encouragement. His head was cocked toward her, his sensuous lips pressed together as though summoning energy to plunder her depths with his kiss.

Her body blazed fire, sending a frisson of ecstasy that she fought to contain. I can do this, she willed, forcing herself to meet his molten gaze. Slowly, carefully, painfully she parted her lips in readiness for his kiss. This is crazy, why am I so afraid, she wondered, as her whole body shook?

"Breathe," she said under her breath. "Breathe. " She met his gaze, thrown slightly by the flicker of vulnerability she detected. A vulnerability that he quickly suppressed as his lips curled into a sardonic smile.

She forced herself not to look away, not to pull back. Her hands were shaking and that irritated her.

'Perfect. That's a shot,' the photographer said. 'You look great together.'

Issy doubted it, but she did know this was the golden hour—casting everyone with a special sun-kissed glow famed for its ability to infuse everyone in a flattering light.

'Just one more for luck and we'll leave you in peace.' He clicked his fingers then waved up the beach.

Issy glanced up as a group of young Fijian men walked toward them playing guitars and ukuleles.

'To get in the mood,' the photographer grinned.

Issy braced herself for what she knew was to come.

The kiss.

'I think this is where you kiss me, *mia cara*,' Max said, grinning like a school boy.

'You want me to kiss you?'

His mouth was so near. She could feel his breath fluttering against her lips, particularly when he said those familiar words, *mia cara,* which she was mortally afraid was some kind of endearment. She was more afraid that she wanted them to be heart-felt endearments, and she was starting down that slippery slope of hope.

If she tipped forward just the tiniest bit she would taste him. She wanted to kiss him as much as she feared it. The push and pull of that made her feel something like seasick, though it wasn't nausea that pooled in her. Not even close. 'I'm not very good at following orders,' she managed to say, 'but you're the boss and if you want me to kiss you—'

'No, Miss Riley,' Max corrected, '*he* wants you to kiss me,' he arched his powerful neck toward the photographer.

Her nostrils flared. Of course she knew it was true, but the sting of his rejection bit nevertheless. Damn that arrogant, insensitive brute. He could at least have pretended to want her.

'The light is going, please focus. This kiss,' the photographer said, impatiently.

God, the pressure.

She looked at Max imploring him to choose another pose. Honeymooners must do more that kiss endlessly. But then what did she know? She'd never even made it to the wedding.

Max's strong arms suddenly curved around her, pulling her toward him before Issy had a chance of protesting, or any hope of escape. She should have been angry, she should have resisted. She should have fought. But she didn't want to.

Behind them the sun blazed like molten gold. She was like liquid in his hands, powerless to resist.

He stood behind her, his powerful chest against her back, his arm on her belly, pressing her to him. His breath was warm on her neck. The sound of the lapping waves against the shore merging with the soft rhythmic sound of the ukuleles and guitars, wafted around them, carried on a warm tropical breeze. The music penetrated her soul as her body melted into his.

She felt on fire as he trailed soft, sensuous kisses along her neck.

Then, when she thought she could wait no more, he spun her toward him. In the swiftest of moments Max's mouth was on hers. His breath tasted of cinnamon and dark chocolate.

'Yes, like that,' the photographer said circling them and snapping the lens in quick succession. 'Don't stop.'

He needn't have asked. She didn't want to stop. Not ever.

She went crazy with longing.

This was a kiss to build a dream on.

Then reality bit. She felt a stab to her heart. She knew this was a test for them both. To show once and for all there was no passion, there was no real feeling, there was no happily ever after.

This kiss would finally end the madness. But rather than quench the thirst, his lips ignited an insatiable one. A deeply fulfilled breath escaped her. He was everything she hoped for. *Everything she didn't need.*

Lust rolled through her in tidal waves of longing. Her body ached with desire to do more than simply kiss.

She breathed a murmur of need. He responded in kind deepening his kiss, pulling her to him. She felt his arousal, powerless to pull away. She rocked against him in unconscious rhythmic motions.

'That was for the camera,' he said, tearing away.

29

What had come over him? Max did not lose control like this. She hadn't seduced him. She hadn't even desired him—it had all been for the camera. And still he had been seconds away from throwing her to the sand and ravishing her in a frenzy of need. She was maddeningly impervious to his sexual prowess. The fact that she seemed not to care just made him want her more.

Max strode down the palm-fringed beach. He had lost control. *Again.* Him. The consummate control freak. He who had unwavering control over everything, every inch of his empire, every electron of his body—until now.

Alien fear made him push away from her, all the way down the sandy beach.

His memory burned with the way she looked at

him with passion clouding her eyes, her lips swollen by his into a cauldron of enticement.

That was for the camera. He couldn't help the harshness of his tone. They'd both been faking it—hadn't they? Why then was he fighting urges that had no place in a life mapped out to the nth degree. Her kiss inspired him, unlocked his creativity—wasn't that all he wanted from her, wasn't that what he had decided? That all roads would lead and stop there?

A flurry of lime and orange snared his attention. He watched feeling unsettled as a pair of Flame Doves swept past him.

Opposites attract. It was chemistry. Biology 101. Testosterone meets estrogen. Nothing more, he mused, striving to make rational sense of it all. In a chemistry lab, yes. But he'd never felt what he had just felt with any of the other women he'd kissed. What was it about this obstinate, willful , woman who was totally opposite to him in every way woman? He gritted his teeth, refusing to admit the blatant proof of his sexual attraction.

I'm a man, he offered, loathing himself for his pathetic excuse.

He raked his hands through his hair. He tried to deny the unpalatable truth. He wanted more. The truth was she was someone he really could care for. The only one his arms liked to hold.

He gazed back to the village, knowing he would be expected for the Kava ceremony. He would have to turn back. He couldn't keep running forever. He picked up a fallen coconut lying on the sand and placed it against a coconut tree. Raising his hand like a sabre he held it over the husk, glancing briefly back toward the village and following the plume of smoke billowing from their fire.

He'd been cruel, lying to her that his kiss was only for the camera. Crueler than he intended. But he couldn't risk the embers of attraction thawing his heart. She wouldn't be able to stand the heat, or the fire that would destroy her when the relationship inevitably went up in flames.

He didn't want her to be burned. Better to be cruel than kind. She'd thank him one day when she married the kind of guy a girl like her deserved. A man that would make her a princess, put her on a pedestal. A man who wouldn't sacrifice their love to a career dedicated to making squillions.

Precision, not emotion, certainly not love—that was his talent, his calling, his métier, his skill, the only thing he did with any aplomb, he mused. Then without flinching, with the speed and force of lightning, he chopped through the air, arching the side of his palm down onto his target.

The coconut snapped in three segments, spilling

the juice inside. He lifted a piece filled with translucent white liquid and lifted it to his lips.

His hard-hearted resolutions sounded good in his head. Why then did his mouth overflow with the taste of her? Every electron in his body did an exultant dance, the air charged with sensuality, as his thoughts turned erotic. Why did his body still want her naked in the sand?

30

'Knock it back.' Max said, his voice a low, hard-edged whisper. 'You'll offend them if you refuse.'

Issy grimaced, staring down into the murky brown sludge, swimming around in the half coconut shell which Tukana handed her. Surrounding her, the villagers seated on the mat for the Kava ceremony looked at her expectantly.

She noticed with rising irritation that Max had not even taken a sip. Obviously, he was afraid of ceding control. *Again.* Afraid of what this murky, beguilingly benign cup of liquid mud could do to his mind. Well, she was afraid too. She'd heard of its potent effects, coiling its way through your senses, your inhibition.

It wouldn't be so bad if it didn't smell so vile. If

she could only distract them all she could tip it out and pretend to enjoy it, as a child she'd had great success with Brussels sprouts, boiled cabbage and any other substance that offended her senses. She'd mastered the disappearing act of politely coughing, while discreetly and with lightning speed slipping the contents of her mouth into her hand, and popping the offenders into the mouth of their ever obliging family dog. But there was no obliging dog now, and everyone had eyes riveted on her.

'Do Fijians drink Kava every day, Tukana?' she said, stalling for time.

'Kava is very popular in Fiji—and the other Pacific Islands. Even the church likes us to drink it—it is much better for our people than alcohol. Better for you too,' he said, shooting her a conspiratorial look, 'I promise.'

Alcohol had never done her any favors, Issy thought, nor had striving to maintain her professionalism, she mused, pressing her lips together to crush the pulsing memory of that kiss and the heated night of passion Max and she had shared.

'Kava is very spiritual,' Tukana added. 'And very important to our artists—fueling the fires of inspiration.' His eyes glistened as though in a heavenly trance.

Spirit and inspiration. Two magnetic words, she thought as she glanced up at the sapphire sky. A million tiny bright stars sparkled like fairy dust. It was a magical night. Thirty or so degrees she guessed and the air was strangely still and calm. The day's lingering heat enveloped her body like their lingering embrace.

'And Kava is very, very relaxing—good for removing stress. In fact, in Fiji there is no word for stress, thank you to Kava.' Tukana said, grinning at Max as he knocked back his third cup.

Issy stared into the murky liquid. She hated that everything reminded her of Max's forbidden passion. Perhaps the Kava would help dull her heightened senses and make her forget.

'Gentlemen before ladies,' Issy said to Max, swirling her coconut cup. 'After all, this is your stress break—the whole purpose of our being here.'

Max looked at her, a devilish quirk on his lips, causing heat to flooding her body. Feeling vulnerable under the intensity of his gaze she forced herself to hold his stare, thinking it would break his hold. But the brute held fast—as though it was an arm wrestle and he was determined to show a strength that deep down he feared he no longer possessed. Could it be that he felt as she did, she wondered?

Tukana chuckled as they stared at each other, 'Already the Kava is weaving a spell.' At this Max looked away, laughing with a tight, shallow, nervous laugh. So he wasn't Mr. Cool, Issy mused, suddenly drawn to his vulnerability. What on earth had made him so wary. What did a man with his looks, his money, his intelligence—a man who on the surface had it all—have to fear?

Tukana began to clap, slow, languid claps with a cupped hand making a hollow sound. The firelight torches surrounding the garden flickered, filling the air with an element of fantasy.

'Bula!' Tukana cried, lifting the shell to his lips, he downed the Kava in one gulp. He emerged smiling, his face serene, his eyes infused with ethereal light.

'Bula!' Issy and Max cried in sync—as though in that moment they both decided to cede control, give up, let go and embrace the unknown.

The foulness of the drink, tasting every inch of the gnarly earthbound root from which it was grown, was sweetened immeasurably by the warmth that fluttered through her heart as she sat cross-legged on the Masi mat beside Max.

She closed her eyes, projecting the memory of that stolen kiss—earthy, sensual, grounding and euphoric all at the same moment, a kiss like Kava that transported the senses, fired inspiration, fueled her imagination.

Kava soaked her lips as she pulled the coconut shell away as at last the drink was gone.

'You're dribbling,' Max trailed his finger in a long sensual movement below her chin, wiping away a trickle of Kava

She rocked her head from side-to-side mutely, unable to speak. Did he have absolutely any idea the havoc his touch reaped?

'My wife has a special gift for you. A couples' Fiji massage. Would you like that?' Tukana said, breaking the silence.

'Yes, we'd like that,' Max said.

Issy's heart thumped heavily in her chest. Really, he'd like that? Besides the fact he'd made it clear he hated relaxing. Any alpha male she'd ever known would want to head to the nearest sports bar, take advantage of any free time with a belly full of beer and an eye on the rugby.

Just what was he up to? Had the Kava taken control of his left brain? Whatever it was, she thought, stretching her feet and wriggling her toes, for once in her life she wasn't going to argue.

31

'How's the pressure, Mr. Balforni?' Kerela asked.

'It's perfect,' Max murmured, barely able to speak as he lay on the massage table, nestled at the edge of the lagoon, cocooned amongst the swaying palms and tropical garden. He lifted his head lazily, glancing at the miles of white sand and azure sea stretching out before him. The magic elixir of coconut oil and frangipani wove a spell as Kerela kneaded the tension from his muscles.

'These ancient aromas and soothing rhythms will help guide you on your journey to serenity and relaxation,' she said.

'*Bene*,' he murmured. Total relaxation took him by surprise as he felt himself drifting off. He couldn't think of the last time he'd felt so relaxed. In fact, before coming to Fiji there hadn't been any time in his life when he'd kicked back and done nothing at all. It felt good, dangerously good.

He turned his head slightly glancing at Issy lying beside him, enjoying her own massage.

Clearly, she was a massage queen, Max thought, as she lay eyes closed beneath the towering coconut palms interspersed with frangipani, hibiscus and bougainvillea flowers. Her skin glowed like a woman who'd just had sex.

Her eyes flickered open, sending a kick to his heart as her giant emerald eyes met his. 'I told you you'd like it,' Issy said, in that sensually familiar voice, oblivious to the turmoil she sent crashing through his veins. He wanted her—because she was so different, or in spite of it, he wanted her. Forcing himself to keep his hands off her since that first frenzied sexual encounter was beginning to be tiresome.

He wouldn't admit it, not to her, but dare he say it, he felt great. The Kava and the massage he affirmed in his mind, not wanting to admit that perhaps it was all because of her.

His muscular tension relieved, his mind and body uplifted from the amazing rhythmic massage. He opted for the deep tissue massage, which promised the manipulating of muscles and tissues reducing body aches and stiffness. It seemed more scientific and physiological, something that allowed him to remain in control. Unlike the fluffy aromatherapy massage that Issy had chosen. But now, it seemed Kerela had gone ahead and mixed an ancient blend.

Who knows what potions were put in that mix.

He glanced over as Issy turned away. Her shoulders and lower back glistened as the moonlight and candles danced over her body. He caught his breath. Not just because she was voluptuous like a woman in a Renaissance painting, but also because she was so refreshingly pure.

Desire lapped his body. For a briefly delicious moment he succumbed surrendering to the fantasy that it was he who was gently massaging her body. He felt the soft sensuousness of her skin, as his fingers followed the contours of her heavenly body. He felt his manhood throb with desire. Max was grateful he was lying on his stomach.

'Not too hard?' Kerela asked, forcing his mind back to the present, as she wrestled with a tight knot locking his shoulders.

'Hard is good,' he said. The firmer Kerela pressed, the less he would fantasize about getting up from the table and taking Issy there and then in a frenzy of unrestrained passion. 'Hard is very good.'

'I can't believe you've never had a massage, ' Issy

murmured, oblivious to the conflict tormenting his mind and body.

How could he tell her that the only time he was ever touched by a woman was when he was firmly in control. Touch to him meant vulnerability. Even in the throes of passion with many of the women he'd bedded it was not the wild passionate love-making of a man who had lost his heart, but of one very much in control of his mind.

How could he tell Issy that she didn't even need to be the one touching him to ignite all his senses. How could he tell her that with her beside him his life was a thousand times richer? That all his senses were heightened in a way no that other woman had ever ignited.

He wanted to tell her she tasted like honey, that she smelt like gardenias, that she felt like a warm tropical breeze, that she looked like a rare luminous pearl. But he told her none of that afraid that he would raise her hopes only to send them crashing upon the jagged rocks of his previous failed relationships.

'Big knots.' Max grimaced as Kerela picked up some smooth river stones, and threw the weight of her body into her arm, sweeping with long fluid movements from his shoulder blade to his neck repeatedly until finally, the muscle relaxed. 'You're very tense.'

If only she could massage the tension from his mind he thought, as, despite all his attempts to cease thinking of Issy, he blazed with impure thoughts about the woman lying nearly naked beside him.

Issy looked like she'd floated off to sea.

'You snored,' he said when her eyes flew open.

She smiled self-consciously, the stars bouncing in reflected light from the sea highlighting the gentle contours of her face. Wide-eyed and entranced, he watched as she arched her feline body, her eyes closed and impervious to his need.

Kerela's sister's dark fingers gently massaged Issy's face, trailing around the voluptuous contours of her mouth. He took a ragged breath, his lips parting. He wouldn't lose control.

Only a foot separated them. All he had to do was reach over and steal a kiss. He was aware of the turmoil of sensuality. The moisture of the massage oil, the heat of the smooth river stones gliding along his body. His eyes flickered and he closed his eyes, surrendering to the fantasy which wove through his mind like an enchantress.

No, he wouldn't lose control. But that didn't mean that they wouldn't be lovers.

32

Dazed, Issy lifted heavy eyelids and. before she could register that he was looking at her, gazed into Max's face. A seductive smile played on his lips that sent her heart pounding. The striking features of his honed-to-perfection face sent a shiver of desire surging through her. For the first time she understood the agonizing power of insatiable need, a power made more potent by the realization that hers was a need that would never be satisfied.

Never again would she taste those lips. Never again would she touch the formidable power of his aroused body.

The air was aflame—the night calls of birds and gentle sea lapping against the shore, the balmy evening breeze ruffling the coconut fronds. It was all so surreal. Here she was virtually naked, save for the thin sheet covering her body, lying next to an equally naked man, and not just any man—a total hunk. This was the stuff of honeymoons.

But, she mused, throwing cold water on her imaginings, she wasn't married and this was no honeymoon. It was work and she had a job to do. Cold, reliable common sense and logic, with which she rarely fraternized, would be her trusted companion.

However much she enjoyed those illicit kisses she was no top-shelf beauty. She was not at all like the sort of woman Max would pursue. Let alone marry. Long limbed, like a gazelle, not a hippopotamus. Blonde sleek hair to her buttocks, not a flamingo pink bird's nest. Need she go on? Why torture herself with the inevitable? He could, and would, have his pick of any supermodel.

Max lifted his head and gave her a smolderingly dangerous look. Issy gazed into his infinite eyes and floated seamlessly into the vast cosmos.

'I'll take the first shower,' she managed, breaking the spell. She slid off the large table and rose to her feet unsteadily. Moving quickly she avoided his gaze, lest he see the desolation in her eyes. How on the planet was she going to get through the next few days?

33

'What's so funny?' she said, suddenly aware of his bemused stare.

'Nothing, I was just admiring you.'

'Admiring me?' she didn't attempt to mask her surprise.

'Just thinking, pinching myself really.'

Her heart hammered.

'To be in one of the most beautiful places on Earth—' he looked at her, unblinking, 'with the most fascinating woman in the world.'

'Must be the Kava,' she blurted tossing the compliment back. At least he hadn't lied and called her beautiful. Captivating was better, safer. Better to reject herself first before he came to his senses.

'How long do the effects of Kava last?' she asked as Kerela walked beside them toward the village.

'I've never seen him like this? He's gone quite mad.' She laughed in spite of herself, realizing with a start she was enjoying seeing this new playful side of him. She didn't tell them she felt lightheaded, happier than she had ever felt in years, her whole life, she corrected. Why did good things have to end?

'It's not the Kava,' Kerela said, smiling as she pointed to the tree. It's *love*.'

Love. The word sat like an undetonated grenade. The tension, the shift in energy, was unmistakable. Both of them froze like a scene in Maxwell Smart. Iron door after iron door slamming down, fortifying, protecting their hearts.

Shaking, she gazed toward where Kerela was pointing

'The Flame Doves,' she laughed, pointing to where the birds were nesting.

Issy felt her heart kick as she recalled what Tukana had said when she'd seen them for the first time. *They take a long time to find a mate, but once united they never part.*

Issy and Max had already united. They were no longer strangers to each other. Not after that steamy night of passion. He'd tasted her just as she could taste him now. She wanted him to taste her again. Mind, body, and soul. If he did, perhaps a miracle might happen. Perhaps he'd realize what she already knew, that there'd be no questions and no need for answers. That their language would be the language of birds.

Except she wasn't a Flame Dove anymore than Max was an orange-crested, long-tailed bird of paradise. In three days they would be forever parted. She would go back to her dingy bedsit and he would gladly return to his opulent life.

She could see Kerela's eyes change, growing as dark as the sky above them.

'You're such a sweet romantic,' she said, remembering with a start these were the words Max had thrown at her once.

Romantic and naive.

She glanced up at the sky noticing a bruised yellow staining the fast banding clouds and started to remind Kerela she was only here to work, that dreams and desires and desires weren't enough. That even though she wanted the fantasy of mating with Max for life to be true more than anything, that her bones were melting from the desire for him, it wasn't enough.

Nerves sprinkled along her skin, all the more frantically because of the relaxing, escapist hour she'd just spent.

The wind blew around her, stirring the trees, stirring her desire.

No amount of lucid dreaming would change the facts.

'You know what real love is?' she said, forcing an optimistic tone. 'That beautiful moonlight massage you planned for us both.'

The bird song which has once filled the air suddenly stopped, replaced instead by the wild roar of the once languid sea, now a swelling wall of fury. The hot, wild wind grew in strength.

The light dimmed. Thunder rumbled.

She could hear Tukana calling, 'Come quickly.'

The grip on her hand was tight as Max pulled her toward the idling Land Rover.

Max leaped in beside her as the sky opened and the rain poured.

'You'll be safer staying here tonight,' Tukana said, glancing out as lightning flashed in wicked bolts.

She jolted back against the seats.

Be careful what you pray for.

34

The Land Rover swung off the road, a sign saying "Happily Ever After" greeting them as they pulled into a gated driveway.

'We took your advice,' Tukana said, ignoring Max's appalled stare. 'And focused on honey-mooners.'

Max shook his head in disbelief. Happily Ever After. How ironic. Having vowed he would never marry, that other than design bridal couture, he would never subject himself to the fairytale fantasies of women, he now found himself literally being driven towards his honeymoon. Was this the villagers' idea of a joke?

His hand-tightened around the car handle, as though impelling him to make a leap to freedom. He was being ridiculous, of course. No woman, no matter how enigmatically compelling, could force him against his will. And with the threat of a cyclone advancing ferociously, this secluded hideaway on the northern most part of the island was as safe, and, for now, as dry as it would get.

'Let's not assume the worst,' Issy said, resorting to the optimism she had so carefully cultivated over the years, 'why don't we just wait to see what they've created. Hopefully there'll be a nice area where we can finally start what I was employed to do,' she said, her brows knitting together as at last the accommodation came into view at last. 'We'll just have to go with the flow.'

Max stiffened. 'I did not turn around a failing business, expand a formidable portfolio of fashion and jewelery lines by going with the flow,' he said, fixing Issy with a reprimanding glare. 'Planning, scheduling, rational analysis, anticipating every single thing that could go wrong and then making sure it never did, that's the measure of success.'

'Well how's that working out for you, ' Issy flashed. 'Would it really have been that hard to have scanned the weather forecast.'

Max slumped back against the seats. Grudgingly he conceded she had a point.

'You sure you two are not married?' Tukana said, chuckling. 'You argue like me and my girl,' he said, giving his wife a wink.

'Go with the flow,' he said. 'It may suit bohemians and bums but it's no way to run a business. Flow does not win business contracts, flow does not create an empire, flow does not create the world's favorite haute couture.' Still, he thought, running a successful empire had taught him one thing—pick your battles.

And right now, he mused, looking up at the moody sky, it looked as though the storm would win.

There were worse ways to spend a night. He stretched out and gave a hearty chuckle.

'Why are you laughing?' asked Issy, thrusting out her chin.

'This is priceless,' he said. 'Milano's most notorious bachelor, Italy's consummate control freak, the world's most unlikely man ever to be hoodwinked by a woman and here I am running from a storm—on my honeymoon with a virtual stranger. But wait, it gets better, the most revered designer in the world, if he survives nature's wrath, is about to spend the next three days playing with paints and crayons. If I didn't laugh I'd probably have a heart attack.'

'If I said I was insulted would you care?'

'Surely you've heard that laughter is one of the best antidotes to stress,' he said sweeping aside her protests. 'Pinch me,' he said, thrusting a muscled arm toward her. 'Pinch me and tell me I'm not hallucinating.'

'Ha. Ha. I'm glad you find it a joke. Personally I find it terrifying,' she said jumping as a loud crack of lightning boomed through the sky.

Her fingers pinched together as her hands clutched his arm. He felt a zing of desire ricochet through his body as she clung to him. Then smiled with satisfaction when her pinch barely registered a mark. Instead of the soft, malleable, dare he say flabby skin of most men her slender fingers met biceps like Italian granite. And in that moment he relished the role of protector.

'Welcome to Lomani,' said Tukana. 'In Fiji Lomani means 'in love,' he said chuckling as he slid from the driver's seat. 'We listened to your marketing advice and thought that would be a winner.'

Max grimaced.

'The setting is exquisite,' Issy said brightly as though forcing herself to think optimistically as she entered the small thatched bure. "Gosh, you've really gone to a lot of trouble—it's enchanting,' she said, taking in her surroundings. 'Gosh, where did you find those cushions shaped like love hearts? They're adorable. And you seem to have them in every possible shade of red. Ohhh, and you've even strung a rainbow of love hearts from the ceiling, and fairy lights.'

The Islanders in their enthusiasm had taken things a little too far, Max thought shading his eyes from the mayhem of discordant color. The over-the-top love nest they'd created was unashamedly tacky and Issy seemed to loved them even more for it.

'Oh, that's beautiful,' she said, taking in the mosquito net of pink silk draped over the marshmallow bed. 'Maybe we can make this work. I could set up my art materials on the deck, I could—' she opened the door, as though hoping to find other rooms, but encountered only an outdoor shower, with two shower heads and towels embossed with a pair of Orange Fruit Doves. 'Where are the other rooms?'

'This is a unique romantic paradise. A couple's retreat,' Tukana said, flashing a while toothy smile.

'We're not a couple. We're not doing romance. You know that,' she said, fixing Tukana with a reproachful stare.

Despite cringing at the decor Max enjoyed watching her strive to keep some semblance of control.

'Couples honeymoon package. That is our target market,' Tukana looked to Max for approval.

'It's all good,' Issy said weakly.

Something dangerous danced in his eyes as Max ambled toward the bed.

'So my bride, what are we going to do now?'

35

———————

He was making her life impossible.

Issy lay on the bed staring up at the love hearts dangling from the mosquito net. A sensual wave of desire fluttered over her as the once gentle rain gained in velocity.

She traced her lips with her finger, closing her eyes and surrendering momentarily to the memory of their night of passion. Her pathetic brain recalling every detail, from the way his eyes glinted gold to the sensuous texture of his beautiful mouth. But since that night, other than that silly honeymoon kiss, he'd been a perfect gentleman.

Emphasis on gentleman, she mused over at him as he lay on the wicker couch. She'd never met a man so cultured and divine—a man that held out her chair, then pushed it in; a man who opened doors for her and now had given up the bed.

She couldn't leave him there, no matter how gallant he had been giving up his own comfort for hers. And she absolutely shouldn't invite him into her bed, but his powerful frame was far too tall for the two person lovebird couch.

Issy let out a long frustrated breath. She would be scrupulously professional, unspeakably detached and utterly sexless. Whatever ideas he may or may not think she was inviting, by morning he'd think he'd been sharing the bed with a rock.

'Come to bed,' she said, aloofly padding over to him. Hopefully, she had injected enough cool detachment into her voice to leave him in no doubt that Passion Down Under was not in the business of providing sex tours

He hesitated—looking more conflicted than fevered with desire. 'I'll take my chances,' he said.

Waves roared toward the shore, as spiraling winds rose in ferocity, coconut trees arched their trunks, bending almost to the floor. Visibility was almost zero as the rain fell in horizontal sheets of water.

He looked at her as though wondering if it would be better to face the eye of the storm than coming to her bed.

'Look, that's my side and this is yours,' she said,

drawing a crease down the middle of the bed. Max's brows furrowed as he looked at the roughly drawn division.

'It doesn't have to be perfect,' she said, noticing for herself without intending it she had given herself a bigger portion. 'I'm a bed hog. What can I say?'

Did his eyes become darker or was it her imagination? 'I normally sleep naked,' he said.

She stared at him.

What I wouldn't give to see that.

'I'm sleeping in my clothes. I'd rather you did too.'

She didn't look at him as she slid under the thin cotton sheets. She heard the soft plop of his clothes landing on the floor. The bed creaked as he lay down beside her. Her foot throbbed with sexy friskiness. She fought against the urge to touch him with her toes to see if he truly was naked. If she closed her eyes and kept them shut, thinking chaste thoughts temptation would be impossible, she told herself. She turned her back to him, feeling awareness swirling between them.

She gave him a cool smile. "Night, Max. '

'*Buona notte,* Isabella.'

She clung to the edge of the bed but despite the distance between them, sparks flew anyway. If they touched he would ignite desire, burning her cotton thin resolve.

While his body was at a safe distance, as safe as it could be in a king-size bed, it was impossible to deny there was a man beside her. A wildly sexy, impossibly attractive man who sent blood surging through her body with no more than a glance.

Issy shuffled a little more to the edge, gripping the side. Any further and she'd fall off. But no matter how much distance she tried to create between them it was as though his aura was fused with hers. It wasn't an auspicious start to the night, but what was she going to say, "Excuse me, can you keep your auric field to yourself."

The room was silent but outside the wind and rain raged. This was a bad idea.

At least he wouldn't be able to hear her thundering heart, she prayed, tensing as a crack of lightning exploded across the sky.

Challenge. That was the best way to look at it. A test of her resolve. A formidable challenge. But she would sleep like a rock, unmoving.

Minutes felt like hours and still they were both awake. She counted sheep, visualized lavender fields, but none of it helped. Normally the strategy from the *Power of Now* book, extolling the virtues of focusing the mind on the sensations of her body, worked a treat.

But not now. Not tonight. Not next to *him*. Her toes yearned to encircle his feet, her chest hammered with an urgent need, her breasts pulsed with desire. She tried to relax all her muscles, think of anything other than what it would be like to be taken by him.

Failing miserably.

There was no other option.

They would have to...

Talk.

'Max.'

'*Si.*'

'You awake?'

'No, *principessa.*'

She pressed her lips together. What other banal things would slide out of her mouth next? Whatever she said, it had to, well, it had to somehow break the aching awareness.

'Would you like me to put my arm around you?' he said, finally bringing his addictive gaze to her. Instead of looking self-conscious, or worse, eager, she frowned at his familiarity.

'Why?' she said thickly, trying to force any treacherous trickle of hope from her voice.

'Because you're shivering, because you jump every time there's thunder, because...'

Issy felt a quick lick of excitement. 'It's all good,' she whispered.

She respected the fact he'd asked her permission. So why was she so disappointed he wasn't offering more? It was darned near impossible to be a rock, she thought as she inched over ever so slightly. A wave of sensual tension locked her body in excruciating rigor mortis as she lay stiffly beside him.

'It could be a long night,' he pointed out. 'The storm sounds like it's only just getting going.'

His eyes were too dark to read. She could feel him searching her face, looking for anguish or fear. The last thing she wanted to look like was a weak and wilting wallflower that needed rescuing.

Oh, but what she wouldn't give for a cuddle. Not that she knew what that would feel like. While she was a great cuddler she'd never been a receiver. Her parents had never cuddled her, not once, and any time a man locked arms around her she'd felt imprisoned. But something about Max's arms looked safe, protective.

She opened her mouth, aching to say, 'Yes please, I'd love a cuddle.' She shook her head and closed it again. She knew only too well where a cuddle would lead.

He looked at her, his face illuminated by the moody violet-tinged moonlight.

Violent gusts of wind arched the coconut trees bending them like rubber bands. Gusts lashed against the shutters, fingers of wind seeped into the room and kicking up the mosquito net that covered them like a wedding veil.

If she hadn't been so tense it would have been incredibly romantic, she mused, avoiding his gaze and staring at the ceiling.

'I thought it was part of your job description,' he said, moving closer.

'What?' Issy said stiffly, sensing the energy shift between them. He was relaxed, playful, in charge.

'To ensure the comfort and relaxation of your clients.'

She stared at him.

'I'm frightened,' he said, grinning, 'frightened and scared. Can you hold me?'

She shrugged. 'Maybe,' she mumbled. The man was impossible. Still, there were worse ways to pass a stormy night... and he was the client, the guest... and he did ask nicely-and he did look so damned cute! 'If you promise to behave.'

He shook his head. 'I can't do that.'

36

Max observed in studied amazement as Issy captured the sunrise with a frenzy of saturated colors. She was sitting on the edge of the cliff, a board and paper on her knees, paints and brushes beside her. The early morning rays as the sun rose above the Pacific captured shades of gold in her tousled hair.

His heart lurched in a way that was becoming disconcertingly familiar every time he was in her presence. He watched as she laid a new blank piece of paper on the pad. Her shoulders tensed, then she crumpled the sketch into a ball, and stared at the horizon with added intensity. Pausing briefly she laid a new blank piece of paper, and began washing it with a yellow glaze, then dropped in pink bands and green circles.

The shapes resembled nothing of the setting before her but seemed to convey her emotions in a way words never could. As scrambled and conflicted as his own He wanted to cry out "A Euro for your thoughts," but he feared what she would say, what she would reveal, what she would ask.

He'd broken his commitment. He'd betrayed his vow. He'd pledged that no woman would ever get close enough to pierce his resolve.What was she really thinking? He had no idea. He barely knew his own mind. Watching Issy as she spontaneously threw down colors onto the page, he , admired and envied her freedom. There was no going by the rules.

He witnessed the moment when her intuition and natural talent took over, and felt a strong, clear surge of clarity about the one thing he could give her. He found himself smiling as her shoulders relaxed, as though concentrating on what was being drawn seemed to release her energy. The picture seemed to be drawing itself on its own.

Occasionally she looked out to the sea, her gaze trailing along the horizon, her thought carried away on the warm sea breeze. He watched mesmerized, confusion reigning over him as she picked up a black pastel, vigorously running it over the vivid colors as though conflicted. But what did he know, he decided, walking toward her. Despite what he felt last night he still knew so little about the language of feeling and emotion. Max walked toward her in a kind of stupor, a shudder going through him, his legs feeling hollow. He was breathing deeply, walking clumsily.

In a crazy flash of untamed longing, in his mind he pictured himself beside her, his arm around her, drawing her in for a kiss, telling her that last night meant more to him than he'd thought possible. More than the squillions in his bank account. Lying beside her he'd suddenly come alive.

But as he drew near, Issy quickly covered the painting with another sheet of paper. She turned to him, biting her lip, a troubled look in her eyes which made his chest hurt. And with that look suddenly all the bravado and aloofness he'd carefully cultivated washed out to sea.

He had stripped naked before her and now he wanted to bare his soul. A fist wormed its way through his chest, pressing against his heart. But instead of closing up, in place of walling himself in, in spite of his apprehension, he wanted to give her everything.

'I want to try—whatever it is that you do,' he said, gesturing to her painting. 'I want to try some of that. Isabella—I need help. I accept that now. I've been blocked. My creativity,' he corrected, fishing clumsily for what he really wanted to say, 'has been blocked. And you're the only one who can help me.'

37

This was good. Very good. Wasn't it? Why then did a worming feeling of dread coil through her chest? All her career she'd battled with cynics, those who thought art-therapy was idle toil. Few recognised its power, deferring their awe to the psychiatrists and doctors who peddled their panacea of magic little pills. Yet art therapy, she had witnessed for herself, was the true healer, the enduring cure.

"It must be nice to do drawing with people," people often said. Nice! She hated the word nice. Didn't people know how hard she worked, attending, listening, ever watchful for the breakout moment, the moment of truth, when people came face to face with their fragmented self, and she, with years of training and skill could throw light on their shadows, illuminate the path away from their private sense of hell.

She shouldn't care what he thought, but she did. She should be delighted that he wanted to embrace art therapy. *Not embrace her.* Shouldn't she? She should be thrilled he saw her as some sort of creative muse, firing the previously low ebb of his creative furnace. Wasn't it better he didn't desire her for who she really was, but respect her for the role he was paying her to play?

Standing up she walked toward him. Her feet felt heavy; her mind full of conflicting emotion, trepidation, fear, loss.

Rejection.

Would he laugh, as others did? Criticize? Dismiss her—pretend to truly engage? She took a deep breath and held her palm to her belly to center herself. No matter what had passed between them, she must set aside her foolish passions and be the professional she knew now, with biting clarity, he had always wanted.

Glancing back at the water she repeated her mantra: "Go with the flow."

Taking a deep breath she pulled out a cane chair, waited for him to sit, then handed him an A3 board. Placing a blank piece of paper on the board she gestured to the tray of crayons on the table.

'You're willing to give this a go but deep down

you think this is childish, am I right?' she said, listening to her intuition telling her where to begin.

He stared at her intensely, arching an eyebrow as though affirming it was not outside the realms of possibility.

'Pick a color for childish.'

His impossibly dark brows creased into a troubled frown. 'A what?'

'A color for childish.' "Pink," she thought as the color flashed through the humid air. "He will pick bubblegum pink."

He rolled his eyes and sighed, gazing out to the lagoon.

'Don't over think it,' she added. 'First thought, best thought.'

He grimaced. Then ploughed his hands into the crayons, withdrawing a bland white one. 'Fluffy,' he growled under his breath. He stared down at the page lost momentarily in his thoughts. Then, he looked at her, a question forming on his tightly pressed lips.

'You can pick more than one color,' she encouraged.

Long, firm fingers grabbed an angry red crayon and scribbled with such fury the table shook, until all the white was consumed by the red, metamorphosing into baby pink.

'Write "fluffy." '

'"Fluffy," there,' he said, pressing firmly and scrawling the word in a flourish. He leaned back, pressing his back against the side of the bure, folding his arms in a triumphant gesture as though relishing the stupidity of the innocuous, non-threatening task.

Good, he was relaxing.

A warm ocean breeze fluttered through her hair lifting the tendrils that fell across her eyes. Feeling eyes upon her she looked up briefly. A tingle of surprise pulsed through her as her eyes rested for several delicious moments on the two Flame Doves hovering in the coconut trees, looking down at them as though absorbed in the therapeutic encounter.

'Tell me about "fluffy,"' she said, deliberately avoiding asking him to write down any *feeling* words. She wagered a bet he'd close up. Experience told her that even the most repressed clients shed their armour when the instructions were less threatening.

'Irritation. Anger. Frustration.' He wrote the words without censure. 'It's damned irresponsible, selfish, undisciplined.'

Without hesitation he picked up a black crayon and scrawled over the word "undisciplined."

'Read what you have written,' she said, keeping her voice soft so it was less a command and more an invitation.

Alpha males like him liked to maintain control and she had perfected the art, professionally anyway, of creating this illusion. She would guide him —but ultimately his unconscious, once tapped, would work the real magic.

'Irritation, anger, frustration ...' his voice grew softer and weaker as he read, as though just naming the words, the emotions, carried them away on the sea breeze. But the real work was just beginning. Something stirred in his psyche, some remembering, some pain he had long repressed.

'Draw irritation.'

'I can't draw with these clumsy things. Give me tools of precision.'

'You told me you wanted to try. Stop trying to control everything.'

He stood mutely silent.

Why was he such a control freak? Telling her what to do, what to wear—and now he had the gall to tell her how to do her work? She took a deep breath and sucked in her frustration. 'It's about thinking differently,' Issy said. 'And to think differently you need to stop thinking. Crayons are a good medium for that. How will you know if you don't give things a chance? If you're not going to be open-minded, if you're not prepared to risk enjoying it more than you'll allow, if you're not prepared to trust.'

'Trust!' he spat the word out like it was a bowl of putrid Kava.

So he didn't do trust, she mused, looking at him carefully, noticing every gesture, every nano movement of his face to see what he might betray.

'Just try!' she encouraged. 'It's not fine art—you don't have to create a Da Vinci or your next couture collection. Even a stick figure or a shape will do. Simply draw irritation.'

'Simply!' he barked, 'You mean childishly,' picking up the red crayon. 'If it's childish you want I can do that fine.'

'It's a big tangled, bloody mess,' he growled.

Scribbling over the page then, as though gripped in a whirlpool, scratching through the words, "Infantile. Frivolous."

He ploughed his hand into the box of crayons, his fingers almost crushed the dark gray crayon he extracted and his eyes blazed with something akin to hatred, "*Disappointing*." pressing so hard the crayon went right through the page. He stared down at the tear, his neck and muscles suddenly rigid.

Max looked up at her. She knew from his expression that he'd revealed more than he cared to. That was the magic—the power to bring the subconscious to light. She took the paper from him and held it in front of her, knowing as she did so he would be drawn deeper and deeper into the drawing.

She felt this anger turn to rage and she could not leave him there. That was, after all, not the point. Her purpose, the conviction that drove her to master this technique, was not to make him vulnerable but to heal wounds buried deep within his psyche. To liberate his spirit and give him the freedom and joy of an unburdened bird.

'Put yourself on the page,' she said, 'Not literally,' she hastened to add, reading his thoughts.

Without hesitating he drew a dark black box, using a ruler from her box of materials, measuring each line precisely.

'I am a grid. I am ordered. Perfect. Flawless. Controlled. Impenetrable,' she noticed his hand shaking.

'It must be hard to control everything, to keep everyone and everything out.'

'It is,' he sighed. 'Exhausting.'

'Pick a wise color. Put some wise words on the page.'

Max picked up a yellow crayon. "Forgive. Forget. Let go. Live."

The color of joy, Issy noted as her heart skipped. But it wasn't her role to analyze but to facilitate. She held up the picture and held it in front of him for a few moments longer than she normally would, knowing it was important to give him time to absorb the new knowledge. He had brought to the surface elements of his past, come face to face with the boy he once was with all his hurts and insecurities. And while she didn't know all the finer details, all that mattered was that something had been brought from the depths of his subconscious to the surface, and now had seen the light.

The sea lapped upon the shore, birds chirped contentedly, the breeze ruffled the coconut fronds as they sat cocooned in silence. At last, he spoke.

'*Grazie mille.*'

38

'The Balforni's weren't my biological parents. I was adopted. Well, fostered really. They never went through with the adoption.'

'But why? I don't understand.'

'I never understood either,' he shrugged. 'Perhaps they just forgot. I decided it didn't matter. They fed and clothed me—or rather the nanny did. And then bundled me off to boarding school when I was four. Surrounded by all these abandoned kids—I don't think I've felt so lonely, so determined to never need anyone's love.'

'That's horrible. Why did they even bother taking you in if they weren't prepared to love you?'

'They'd been trying to adopt for years. They'd given up on having a baby of their own. Then three months after I arrived, my mother fell pregnant. 12

months later my brother, Stephano was born. But my brother died. Cot death. My mother, understandably, was heartbroken. She never stopped grieving—not until Sophia was born four years later. But I'd been banished by then. I guess I reminded her of the baby she couldn't have. Who knows? All I know is that I was a constant disappointment. I determined from an early age I would make them proud of me, that I would make something of my life. If I'd known then how hard it would be to meet my father's expectations—to say he was disappointed is putting it mildly.'

'What more could he possibly have wanted? In a short period, you've amassed a lifetime of artistic recognition. You're the king of the fashion world.'

'I'm a girl.' His gaze, brimming with pain, touched hers then moved away.

'What?'

'My father believed all men involved in fashion to be gay.'

'But that's absurd. And anyway what does it matter?'

'It mattered to him. He was embarrassed by me.'

'So you—'

'So I tried harder. Worked harder. Tried to please my father more.'

'So you stripped all the color from your palette,

all the "childish" whimsy, and frivolity he despised?' she said, understanding catching her heart.

'Yes, and I tried to be more like someone he admired. Someone exactly like him. My father loved women, his philandering ways were legendary. I tried to be like him and paraded a succession of women to family gatherings, each one more beautiful than the last. But they all left me feeling cold. None lasted more than a season. I wondered if he was right. Maybe I was gay. Only I didn't fancy men. No way. So that left me even more determined to pour my heart into my work. And I resolved never to ever feel again.'

'And how did that work out for you?'

'Fine—until you showed up.' He gave a shrug. 'Not one of them made me feel— the way you make me *feel*.'

39

'Wow. That was powerful stuff. I misjudged you. You're like a silent assassin, a psychological sniper.'

'I've been called many things, but I'd have to say that's a first,' Issy said, heart thumping. Secretly pleased that he respected her craft.

'So, art therapist? With your talent for painting you could have been a artist. You still could.'

'Life had other plans for me.' She pressed her lips together, wondering how much to reveal. Did she really want her past to define her. All the failed relationships? Would he judge her. Screw it. So what if he did. Then he was no better than all the other men who couldn't handle her imperfections.

Besides he'd revealed himself to her. Not in that way, she censored, firmly pushing aside a wilfully erotic image of him standing naked before her. He'd been naked psychologically and that demanded reciprocity.

'I'd dreamt about being an artist as a child, having my own gallery, everything. I could see it so clearly. The paintings—not little ones, but big juicy vibrant ones like Rothko's. Paintings that made people sing and offered then a window into another world. But that was before—'

'Before?'

She could almost feel his curiosity smoking between them. No man had ever given her his undivided attention before. She was the one who always did the listening, the counselling, the healing. Feeling awkward, she forced herself to continue.

'Before—' God, she'd have to say the toad's name. Something she'd promised herself she never would. 'Before James.' She drew a deep breath, feeling her heart tighten, and the knots in her stomach.

'We were going to get married. Married by Christmas in fact. Stupid idea. I mean, really.' She painted a tight smile on her lips and willed herself to look at Max to show she really didn't care, that it was done and dusted, her failed relationship a distant memory. But the way he looked at her, as though sharing her hurtful betrayal, like reading an empathetic telegraph wired from her heart to his, told her from this one man she could never hide her true feelings.

'What about you? What's the most emotionally significant relationship you're ever had? Describe your most vivid memory.'

'We were talking about you,' he said.

Crap. Normally diversion worked a treat. But she sensed it was him that was doing the diverting, and the progress he'd already made would deepen if she shared more about herself. 'Um. Well there's nothing to say really. He cheated on me. It could have been worse. I could have been a walking cliché - dumped at the alter. At least he spared me that.'

'Are you always so optimistic? He hurt you.'

Don't cry. Don't you dare cry. 'I got over it. My work helped.'

'We have that in common,' he said.

'Yeah, how ironic,' she gave a weak smile. 'In my line of work they call it the 'helpers high.' Helping other people who are miserable or worse off than yourself actually makes you feel better about your own life. Not just that of course—it's nice to feel you're doing something to make the world a better place.'

Issy felt her shoulders knot, waiting for a barrage of criticism. Do-gooder. What makes you think you can tell other people how to live? You think you're better than everyone else, and all the other mean taunts family and unhappy friends had lobbed at her over the years. But instead he smiled.

'You're a good person, Issy Riley, a breath of lovely fresh air. Promise me you'll never change.'

She looked away, suddenly overwhelmed. 'Okay,' she said, softly hoping he wouldn't detect emotion blocking her windpipe.

'I mean it, Issy. You're not just likeable, you're lovable.'

'Okay.' She studied a spot on the ground. Could it be he cares for me? That at last she could be herself, vulnerabilities and all. An unwanted sense of foreboding gripped her heart. She steeled herself for the inevitable.

'Someday you're going to meet a guy who deserves you,' he said.

Issy opened her mouth to object. She wanted to say, "You. Why can't it be you?"

But instead she said, lamely, 'Okay.'

40

———

'What about you? What about your family?' Max asked.

'We're not close.'

'Really?' he said quietly.

'A boarding school survivor too?'

'No. I wasn't physically abandoned,' she shrugged. 'What can I say? I just didn't fit in. I'm sure I was adopted.' Why else had she been so emotionally abandoned—treated like a modern day Cinderella. 'I tried to be what they wanted, I just couldn't figure out how to make it stick.'

She'd tried so hard for so long, always being helpful, always being agreeable, always quiet, never hogging the limelight. Trying not to excel, or attract attention or any one of the million things that drove her mother wild. It was never enough. She was never good enough. They hadn't wanted her or loved her. 'It wasn't their fault. My mother did her best.'

'You're too kind. They should have loved you.' There was a long pause. 'You're not just likeable—you're lovable,' he said quietly.

She gulped. 'Why?'

'The work you do with kids – I respect you for that.'

Oh, so that was it. He respected her professionally. She swallowed the metallic taste of disappointment. Yet she pondered what he'd told her, couldn't stop prying into his personal life. 'Is that why you're not married? Is that why you don't have children?'

'Partly. I love my work—there's no room for a wife. If I get married I want to do it properly. I want to know it's going to last,' he said, staring at her intensely.

'I know. If that was on the cards for me I'd want the same. I'd definitely be the kind of parent who enabled my child's dreams. I have the blueprints of what not to do.'

He nodded in agreement. 'What if I could enable your dreams? What would you wish for?'

I'd wish for you. I'd wish you knew how I felt. I wish I was brave enough to tell you that I can't stop loving you/falling in love with you.

'I'd wish I was brave enough to expose my work in a gallery one day.'

His eyes glistened, widening into big azure pools of delight, as though the idea excited him. Then he looked at her with such intensity she thought her soul would burst.

'Nothing else?'

'Nope.' she lied.

'Why no ring?" He lifted her hand, sending a tsunami of longing flowing through her.

'I dunno.' Issy pulled her hand away and flicked at her nails. Suddenly she wanted to open up to him. To risk telling him things that would make him walk away, stay away. 'You'll probably think I'm a train-wreck. I've had rings. Plenty of them. But after a while, they end up losing their shine. Know what I mean? I don't care for fool's gold anymore.'

He said nothing, just sat, looking at her in such a way that she suddenly didn't want to hide anything from him anymore.

'First prize, someone says they love you. Second prize a ring. Third prize, they disappear into the arms of another.'

'Good job.'

'What?'

'Well if they're not loyal you're better off knowing that before you get married. Marriage is sacrosanct. It's forever.'

'Is that why you never got married?'

'I'm not marriage material.' he said, his tone hinting at some truth he didn't wish to reveal. 'At least you're not afraid to commit.'

Issy laughed. 'I should be. Relationships just seem so transitory. Maybe it's me. Maybe I was looking for love in the arms of all the wrong men.'

'I thought, geeze, Issy, you're 27—we're talking five years ago—you really have to get your crap together. So I tried to love someone who I thought would be good for me. Enter James. An investment banker—practical, grounded, conservative—he ticked all the boxes. Or at least I thought he did.'

'Boring – he sounds boring.'

Issy laughed. 'Yeah, he was pretty painful.' She bit her lip. But I really wanted kids. And I thought he would be a good provider, a great dad. So when he asked me to marry him, I thought why not? I always dreamt that one day I'd find myself in some field somewhere, standing on grass, and it's raining, and I'm with the person I really, really love. And he really, really loves me back.'

'So what happened?'

'I tried to be what I thought he wanted. To fit in, I changed my clothes, my hair ... .'

'You mean pink's not your natural color?'

'This?' she said, trailing her fingers through her hair. 'This is Push-off pink—that's what I call it. The color I chose when it all crashed and burned. It couldn't have been more spectacular.'

'I know this sounds corny, but all I ever wanted was to be cherished. I wanted to be loved for me. But mostly I wanted a promise keeper.' She shrugged. 'I wanted the impossible.'

'You're zany. You're unpredictable. You're fabulous. I love that you're someone who is anything but perfect. Don't change for any man. You're wonderful. Any man would be lucky to have you.'

'Any man but you?' Her thoughts blurted forth before she could reign them in.

'What?'

'Forget it, I was just being provocative. There's no way we'd work. We're opposite in every way. I'm chalk and you're mozzarella.'

'Opposites attract, *mia cara,*' he said, as the energy sparked, and cracked, and hissed between them

'There must be a reason for that.'

41

'Marry me.' The words spun out of his smiling mouth before his mind could censor. Like a riderless horse, his passion had run away from him. For the first time in years' he'd happily let it run free. He couldn't stop grinning as he waited for her response.

Issy looked up at him. Her eyes once dreamy now flared wide. 'What—did you say? He saw her body stiffen as though every cell of her body were afraid.

'Marry me.'

'Why?' she stammered.

'*Why*?' Why was she asking so many questions? A sinking feeling invaded his gut. He tightened his clasp as she tried to pull away. 'In these last few days you've given me my life back.'

'How? You said it yourself, we're opposites in every way. I'm chaotic, you love structure. I'm late and you're early, I'm talk and you're silence.'

He brought his mouth down upon her doubting lips, needing to know that she felt the way he felt. Fire exploded around them as his tongue met hers, devouring every protest. A thrill of electricity jack-knifed between them as she yielded to him, melting momentarily in his arms.

Her eyes welled with tears. She pulled her hand away, pressing it against her mouth.

'You don't have to do this. You don't have to feel sorry for me.'

'*Te amo*,' he said. 'I love you.'

'No, you don't love me. Not for me. You love me as your muse. You love me because I've given you back your creativity. But I want more. I don't want to be paraded, draped in your designs, relegated to a muse whose only purpose is to penetrate and stimulate your creativity, to bring forth ideas from the womb of your mind, to give birth to nothing but frocks and necklaces and buildings. Because I, stupid fool that I am, love you and I want to live in your heart.'

'My work is everything,' he heard the emptiness in his words, and wished he hadn't spoken. It was him that was the fool.

'And what about my work? What about my ambitions? My dreams? Are they to be relegated to the back seat because your needs come first. Name me one muse who is famous for her creativity.'

'I didn't know you wanted to be famous.'

'That's not the point. I just don't want to be forgotten, devoured by your work, useful only to be the midwife to your creative babies. I want real babies. Your babies.'

'I didn't know—you never said.'

She paused. 'You never asked.'

'I'm asking now.'

'It's too late. You don't mean it.' She took a ragged breath and turned from him, tears streaming down her cheeks. 'I can't be the woman you want.'

42

'You did what?' Nancy blurted down the phone.

'I told you,' Issy said, trying to mask the defensiveness in her voice.

'If you told me a hundred times I wouldn't believe it. But tell me again.'

'Getting him to express his feelings had been the sole purpose of the trip—it's what Passion Down Under tours was about, right? It's why I was drawn here to work as an art therapist. I just didn't think he'd propose. I mean, sure I dreamed about. But it's a fantasy, right? I mean, I can't just go waltzing into his glamor life, can I?'

Issy sat beneath the starry sky, wrapped beneath a black velvet cloak of aloneness. 'Oh, God. Let's face it—when it comes to relationships I'm a train wreck.' Here she was on Christmas Eve in one of the most beautiful, most romantic places on earth and she had no one to share it with. 'I'm a fool aren't I, Nancy?'

'That's putting it mildly! You rejected the guy. Not just any guy—but one of the world's sexiest, wealthiest and, from what you've told me, kindest billionaire bachelors. The guy's a keeper. But you, Issy Jane Riley, push *eject*.' Nancy sighed. 'Have you completely lost your mind?'

'Here I am in paradise on one of the most beautiful nights of the year – alone with a can of Pringles, and a glass of diet Coke. I've fucked up, haven't I?'

'Yip. Geeze, how did the poor guy handle it?'

'He confirmed my suspicions.'

'Your suspicions.'

'He laughed. Told me he was just kidding around. That he's only asked me because he felt sorry for me.'

'And you believed him?'

'Why wouldn't I? Look, I'm no oil painting, I'm at least four dress sizes bigger than most of the stick-insect models he dates—'

'Has anyone told you, you're impossible. You're a goddess of beauty. You are a wondrously beautiful being of light, a creative woman, a spiritual woman, a generous woman—you have everything going for you. Everything. There is nothing to change or fix. A guy like Max would be lucky to have you. And he knows it. And it's time you knew it too. Stop running yourself down. Just be yourself, just love and accept yourself as you are.'

Issy shrugged and pressed her phone to her ear, picking out some Pringles with her free hand.

'So where is he now?'

'At the local village, with Tukana and his family. They're having a Christmas Eve party.'

'Go Issy. Go!'

43

'Issy. You came!' Tukana said, spotting her hovering self-consciously at the edge of the village. 'Come. Come drink Kava and then we shall dance.'

Kava sounded like a great idea, she thought, searching through the Fijians seated on traditional woven mats under the stars for the one familiar face she realized with a sting she longed to see.

'Where is Max?' she asked, injecting her voice with what she hoped would be taken for disinterest. If she was going to stick her neck out trying to win his affection better keep it a private affair. She wasn't a hundred percent certain he would accept her, not after her stinging rejection. Not fifty percent. Not even twenty percent. The man had turned into an emotional refrigerator.

Where was he, she wondered, her heart filling with disappointment as she sat down beside Tukana? She grasped the hollowed half of a coconut he passed her and drank the murky liquid, as approving eyes nodded to the sound of three deep claps.

The Kava was stronger than she remembered and she felt her mouth tingle then go numb. Almost instantly she was handed another Kava and she noticed it had come from the Chief's bowl—a large ornately carved wooden bowl which sat on three short wooden legs in front of him.

'The chief says it's been an honor to have you both in our village,' Tukana said.

His words were said so thoughtfully and earnestly anyone overhearing them would have thought she was the Queen.

'It's me who's been honored,' she said. 'I am only sorry to be leaving.'

'He is a marked man,' Tukana said, nodding to the left of them, where a group was dancing.

'Sorry?'

'Max. All the women of the village want to dance with him. He has been dancing all night.'

Max dancing? She followed his gaze. There was nothing to explain the sudden surge of jealousy. It was an innately primitive response, entirely out of character and out of order given that to all intents and purposes she was still his employee—her only purpose to get him through a particularly stressful time.

Max didn't look in the least bit stressed now, she judged, feeling a stabbing pain in her chest, her adrenaline racing as she watched him sway his far too sexy cotton-clad butt to the music, smiling broadly at the young Fijian woman who smiled equally broadly back. Unlike many of the other Fijian girls with their tight springs of wiry black hair, her hair fell down her back in a cascade of silken black ending where his hand pressed gently on the small of her back as he guided her into a twirl.

She laughed with the confidence of a young woman who, as the other women watching her admiringly also knew, was in the dawn of her youth—her beauty a bud ready to burst into flower. A girl with her looks could easily be Italy's Next Top Model.

Issy turned to leave, feeling suddenly old and frumpy—what the hell had she been thinking? Suddenly a handsome young Fijian man in a cheery pink top scattered with lemon hibiscus flowers approached her.

'Would you like to dance?' he said gently. Unlike the Fijian women with their air of confidence and willingness to take the lead he appeared a little hesitant.

Around them, men sat cross-legged drinking Kava and smiling approvingly.

The music played by local men who, after finding success in Australia, had returned for Christmas to the village. Their sound was powerful and spiritual, sung deep from the heart. Although loud, courtesy of the amplifier the village had recently purchased following a successful fundraising trip to Melbourne, the lyrics and beat had none of the irritating bass and angry angst laden words that characterized so much of Western music.

It was enticing and invigorating, and whether it was this or the Kava suddenly taking effect, Issy agreed to his request.

Why not, she thought, fighting a smidgen of self-conscious paralysis? If Max could loosen up, let himself relax, chillax, she was allowed to dance and have fun too.

'I'd love to,' and she walked with him to the center of the floor feeling 'ridiculously free'. She closed her eyes and let the music take her. She danced like she'd never been hurt, letting the music wash all the disappointment and pain of the last year away. And she was smiling too as she raised her arms like everyone else and threw her head back and let her body move to the rhythm.

And she danced and worked hard to have fun, ignoring the small nagging part of her that wished she was dancing with Max.

44

It was his fault. He'd been the dumbnut to rush things. He'd blurted it out in a reckless sort of spontaneity, only to realize he was deadly serious. He wanted to marry Issy Riley more than anything in the world. There was no point analyzing, or rationalising, or any other rational tool upon wish he had always staked his future. Like the Fijian heat, love had been inescapable. He had not sought it, not chosen it, but now, dare he admit it, he'd got used to it and didn't want to ever go back to the cold.

The cold of a bed devoid of love, the cold of a ballooning bank balance with no wife or children of his own to share it with, the cold of a calculating, at times soulless commercially driven fashion world devoid of the balance a wife and children at home.

Something he knew with punching certainty Issy would bring.

And now she was with dancing with another man, and it took a superhuman effort not to stride through the crowd of dancers and drag her away like a prehistoric caveman taking his woman.

Did it make it better or worse that she wasn't even looking at him?

Better, he decided, and then thought that, no, actually it made things infinitely worse.

He told himself she was just dancing, as were about one hundred other people around her, but then the music slowed and the change in the tempo of the music immediately charged the atmosphere.

The dancing shifted from impersonal to personal as the voices and lyrics reached deep into what—if he believed in such a thing—he would call his soul. Something deeply moving penetrated parts of his psyche he'd long thought dead.

The musicians and crowd swayed from side to side like coconut fronds in a warm breeze.

Max watched through narrowed eyes as hands curved into the centre of Issy's back. That smooth, bare back that had been distracting him all evening.

Max had a sudden image of the flickering of flames of the torches scattered around the garden throwing a bewitching firelight on her soft skin that night he had first claimed her as his own. Suddenly he was striding toward her, snaking past entwined couples, until he reached his target.

If he'd been asked to explain his behavior he couldn't have done so. Not once had he ever pursued a woman and never had he cared enough about a woman to extract her from the clutches of another.

He would fight for her, if it came to that. She was his woman. He was her man.

'My dance,' he said without hesitation. The Fijian man, sensing it was a command not a request, acknowledged it with a reluctant smile and a nod of the head, as he dropped his hand from Issy's hip and backed away.

'Perhaps I'll have the next dance,' he murmured, and Max felt his mood grow darker.

'I've got the next dance covered, and the ones after that.'

45

___

Issy went to object, but closed her mouth, swallowing a strange honey-taste of pleasure, as his hand slid around her waist and pulled her against him before she could object. Suddenly she didn't mind being controlled. She liked the assertive way he held her as though claiming her.

She folded into his chest, her body molding into his with the familiarity of a favorite leather chair, the imprint of the intimacy they'd shared growing strong.

They were surrounded by people, and yet they might as well have been alone for all the difference it made to the attraction.

Their bodies already knew each other, the re- membrance was there and with it the scorching memories. And she felt the sparks ignite between them. It was no longer a simple dance. This time it was forever.

The music stopped and they stood staring at each other. Before the band had a chance to kick into their next set he grabbed her wrist. 'Come on, let's get out of here.'

She felt her pulse flutter against his fingers as he guided her off the dance floor in long confident strides.

'What's the hurry?'

'I won't accept no.' He lifted her face, cupping her chin beneath his fingers. She lifted her eyes to his, emerald green eyes where the past, future, and present melded into one. 'I know you're frightened. I'm frightened too. I can't give you guarantees but all I know with certainty is that I love you. Can't you see that? How many times do I have to tell you?'

'Tell me again,' she whispered, brushing a lock of hair from her face.

'*Te amo, mia principessa.*'

'I was stupid,' she said, her voice quivering, her lips parting softly, the moisture of the hot balmy evening making her skin glow. 'What we ...'

Before she could say anything more he lowered his head and pressed his lips to hers, smothering her explanations in a smoldering kiss.

He felt her trembling heart beat against his as her body folded into his. She lifted her arms and locked them around his neck as he kissed her again and again under the sparkling stars.

As they pulled apart she was smiling and he was smiling too. He took her hand in his and pressing her fingers to his lips kissed them, and reached into his pocket. He withdrew a chain of tiny flowers he'd made into a ring, realizing with a start that never before, with no other woman, had he made such a romantic gesture.

'Isabella Riley, he said, bending on his knee, 'will you do me the honor of becoming my queen.'

She nodded, tears streaking her face, as at last, she spoke the words he never thought she'd say. 'I will. I do. Yes! Yes! Yes!'

Nothing existed but the two of them. He slipped the ring onto her finger, oblivious to the people who had gathered around them.

'We prayed for you,' Kerela whispered stepping forth and wrapping fragrant wreaths around their necks.

'Thank you,' Max said, as Tukana wrapped them both in a large Masi cloth. In a frenzied climax of passion Max kissed her again, this time his tongue probing deep inside her mouth, which tasted not of Kava but a sweet blend of passionfruit mango and, like a bee to honey, he wanted to drink her nectar all night long.

Their lips still locked, their bodies bound by the

Masi cloth, they began to walk through the long grass towards the beach and while the walking kiss did take some skill it felt amazing. How had this one crazy, whacky creative, so-not like his other conquests stolen his heart so? He was acting completely out of type – like the lovesick teenager he'd never been.

'Passion down under,' he laughed, gently slipping his lips from hers.

'Yes, you get the full package—with a complimentary upgrade. But not until our wedding night,' she laughed. 'Seriously... I thought ...'

'Don't think.' Max said. 'You taught me that. Just be in the moment. Go with the flow.'

'... I taught you that?'

'Feelings...'

'Feelings?'

'Like these,' he lifted her hand to his chest, her tentative fingers hesitating from resting upon his heart. 'You, Isabella Balforni, have given me back my childhood.'

Happiness exploded inside her like fireworks, incandescent, as brightly colored as her future.

And then the rain fell in a soft misty veil. And she was standing in a field of grass with the man she loved. Just as she had always dreamed.

46

That night as they lay together in the marshmallow bed Issy let her hands curl over Max's bare shoulders as his mouth slid to her neck, softly biting and suckling her sensitive skin. Though she could feel the force of his desire, he let her set the pace this time, this more important time.

Her breath was unsteady as her fingers traced the thin vein of scar tissue snaking across his heart. There was raw, vulnerable power there, she'd wanted to feel it, but had been afraid to. Issy could hardly believe she was touching the man who would soon be her husband.

A gentle tropical rain danced on the thatched straw.

Max lay motionless smiling, but his skin quivered with longing. He gazed at her with a love so consuming the bed suddenly seemed too large, the night too short, the days too few.

'Make love to me, Max.'

The words were barely formed on her lips when he drew her toward him and kissed her again. This time as his mouth touched hers he kissed her with such feeling, such warmth, such tenderness that all her inhibitions disappeared. She folded into the softness of his lips, no longer holding back her heart.

Carefully, as though afraid to make the wrong move and ruin it for them both, he slid his hands under her cotton nightshirt, up her belly, then cupped her breasts in slow, agonizingly aching movements. His sultry masculine scent and his power were an aphrodisiac she no longer wanted to resist. She writhed in the sheets, bursting with need, as commanding, sensual fingers encircled her nipples—following the rise of them as they hardened with urgent desire.

She moaned, long and low—no longer worried about keeping the unmistakably sexual sound inside. A small critical voice tried to tell her she should be silent. A much stronger voice, the one he'd woken with that first kiss, insisted that with this one man she was free to expose her deepest feelings.

He hesitated, gazing deep into her eyes. '*Mia ten-tatrice,*' he whispered. If there was a sexier sound in the world she'd never heard it. Sensing that her longing met his ten-fold Max pulled her nightshirt over her head with quick powerful tugs. The cotton dragged across her aching breasts, over her lips, over her eyes. Her fingers clutched the soft, fine cotton of the bed linen, winding around the sheets, as he kissed her breasts.

Her hands wrapped around his broad neck, then slid down his back, reveling in the feel of the sculpted muscles bunching under her touch.

She was no longer a rock. She was an island, and he was the sea pummeling against her in rhythmic, explosive movements as his strong, warm chest pressed against her breasts. He slid down and kissed her belly, her hips—stopping only when his lips rested in the shallow valley between her woman-hood and the inside of her legs, his tongue barely tasting the underside of that one curve. His mouth stayed there, tempting, taunting her with what it might do next.

Warmth and longing flooded her being, delight increasing the sexual need thumping through her.

She suddenly found herself breathing fast. 'Make love *with* me, Massimiliano.'

He drew away, only far enough so that they could see each other. His eyes searched her, confirming what they knew. This was what they both wanted. What they both needed. What they both desired. This was a night they would always remember. A night they would never forget, the first night of many nights for the rest of their lives.

His lips curved. Their hearts opened. Then his hands were framing her face, and he was kissing her so gently every cell in her body felt drugged. She shuddered against him. For the first time in her life, she felt beautiful and adored.

Something danced inside her, whispering that she was as beautiful as he was, as powerful. She arched her back and then surrendered herself to his talented hands, as he slid his mouth from her lips.

His sensitive fingers spread her legs teasingly slowly, causing every millimeter of skin he touched to scorch from each spark that lit her nerve endings.

His powerful hands felt so strong, so firm, yet his fingers rubbed her with the delicacy of a jeweler polishing a rare gem.

'*Te amo,*' he murmured. He lifted her against him with a display of superior strength, attuned to her every response, nurturing it, heightening it.

'I love you too,' she said huskily. Her breathing was ragged as at last, he gave her what she ached for. His rhythmic thrusts, sensual and possessive, washed her body with vivid, explosive colors, waking her up after years of being asleep to her own sensuality. He plunged into her, unleashing the force of his passion. A deep groan rolled through her like a quake of thunder. She felt him explode, and the power sang through her, losing her in a sensation too deep, too vital, too impossible to define, too magical to comprehend.

More than passion. More than desire. More than love.

THE LOVE HEARTS fluttered in the breeze as they lay beneath pink silk netting. 'It was love at first sight. A love that would last a lifetime. I knew it the moment I saw you rescuing the snake. Only I didn't trust it. I couldn't believe it. The feeling was so foreign, unknown, unexpected—beyond my wildest hopes.' Issy snuggled into his comforting arms.

'I'd almost given up on love, and then there you came like a Templar Knight to the rescue. Before I met you I'd been lost, incomplete—only I didn't know it. In one instant you took possession of my heart,' she lay her head upon his pounding heart. 'I know it now. I've loved you forever, we just had to meet.'

'It was the same for me, my darling. *Te amo,*' he said, 'I love you.'

She felt tears starting to fall as she stared into

his eyes. The depth of emotion she saw, she was certain was mirrored in her own.

Issy felt like she could fly, and she knew with joyous certainty that they both knew what they felt would last for life.

47

———————

'Married by Christmas? But that's tomorrow! I know I said to go for it, but isn't that a bit quick?' Nancy blurted down the phone.

'Sometimes you just know, Nancy. You just really know,' Issy said, dragging great gulps of air. 'I know it sounds crazy. I can't believe it myself.'

'Yes, but—oh, Issy. I know I encouraged you. But what if you get hurt again? What if it's all my fault?'

'I want to live fearlessly, Nancy. I'd rather take another chance on love than spend a lifetime of regret. Besides, I wasted five of my best childbearing years waiting for James to get his act together, then a week out from our wedding day. Bam. Jilted. I know better than anyone that that love doesn't come with guarantees. But this time—this time I just know. Massimilliano Balforni is a promise keeper.'

'Are you happy?'

'Madly.'

'Then I'm happy for you. Even if I'm pissed off I don't get to be a bridesmaid.'

'Well, here's the thing, you still do.'

'What? You mean? Really?'

'Yes!' Issy giggled, hearing the thrill of excitement in her best friends voice. 'Of course I wouldn't get married without you. I mean, you're practically my sister! So we're getting married twice. We're tying the knot here in Fiji tomorrow, Christmas Day. We're having a terribly intimate ceremony in the sweetest little church, and then flying out to Milan for a big fat Italian wedding.'

'Oh, my God. Where?'

'At the Milan Cathedral! The Duomo! I've been helping and Max is designing an extra special dress in blazing red, with a huge train, and loads of ruffles, just like the one he saw in the watercolor I painted,' she gasped, barely pausing for air. 'And he's designing a massive green sapphire engagement ring. I told him I don't need all those expensive things,' she said, looking down at the ring he'd made from flowers, but he said the ring he gives me needs to last.'

'I hate you. No! I really hate you.' Nancy laughed.

'You'll be bridesmaid—the only one. Just like when Wills married Kate. And some hot Italian guy's going to see you looking so beautiful in one of Max's couture dresses and he'll step right out of the crowd and ask you to marry him. And we'll both be married and our kids will grow up together. Oh, Nancy—I know it all sounds crazy. My arms are bruised from pinching myself. It's like a fairytale. But for the first time in my life I know that dreams can come true.'

'See, didn't I always say that one day you'd meet your prince?'

'Something tells me we're both going to get our happy ever after.'

EPILOGUE

'*Il principino o la principessina potrebbero arrivare a giorni,*' Max, said, bending over to kiss Issy's bump, as they sat surrounded by her giant sized paintings in the Isabella Gallery in Milan .'Like its mother, the baby is late.'

'If she is a girl we will call her Isabella, after her beautiful *mamma.*'

'And if he is a boy, Massimo, after his handsome father,' Issy laughed.

'Promise me we will have many children, *cara*?'

'You're impossible,' she laughed. 'But, yes, after my next exhibition. I can't believe my paintings all sold. Oh, my God, the prices! Amazing. Without you —', she said, wrapping her arms around his waist and hugging him—without your belief in me this never would have been possible.'

She spun around the gallery he had created for her, glancing toward the painting entitled, "Flame Doves." Painted in a riotous blaze of orange and limes, fuchsias and pinks, it captured everything she felt, and she was glad as she looked at the catalog dotted with red "sold" stickers, that it was going to an art collector with deep pockets who loved the painting as much as she did. She would send all the money to the lovely young woman who had taken the helm of Issy's Kids.

'I want a big family—a big gorgeous, loving family. And I agree with you, our next collection, my paintings, and your new fashion line must capture the joyfulness children bring,' she said.

'*Assolutamente,*' Max said, drawing her to his side. 'We'll do all we can to stop our babies from growing up too fast. They will stay little *principino o la principessina* as long as they can.'

Issy's freckled face shone with love as she looked at him with those infinite eyes that had snared his heart from the moment they'd met. He ran his hand over his broad chest, fingering momentarily the fine scar lying across his heart. If he was any happier, he thought, his heart might break. '*Te amo. Te amo. Te amo,*' he repeated. 'I love you to infinity and back.'

He bent and kissed her, savoring the sweet taste of her lips. 'You know how they say, "You just know"? I just knew. I still do.'

. . .

LATER THAT NIGHT, lying in Max's arms, she thought happily that they'd both taken a chance on love again and had won the lottery.

At last, she belonged. Home truly was where the heart was, and her heart belonged with Max. He was everything she ever needed without being consciously aware of it. No checklists, no profiling, no prescriptive analytical criteria. Just feelings. Just her heart. Just love. He was simply perfect. With him, she didn't need to pretend. She could be her true crazy, chaotic self.

Now she understood. They were destined to be together. Their childhood traumas, their insecurities, their emotions, buried and hidden from others, they had both been searching for the missing piece in their lives, only to find it in each other.

'Kiss me,' he commanded in a voice both rough and tender.

'I'd love to,' she murmured, lifting her face to his, knowing that each kiss was forever.

THE END

AUTHOR'S NOTE

The idea for this story was sparked when I read about a very successful Italian fashion-tycoon who said, 'My biggest regret is that I gave my life to my job.' It struck me as very, very sad.

I wondered why he had chosen to live his life this way. Despite all his wealth, all his mansions around the world, and all the 'fans' who adored him for the identity he had carefully cultivated, he loved no one and no one loved him back for who he truly was.

Although he never said it outright, he'd thrown himself into his work following the death of his life partner. His work was pure escapism—protecting him from feeling the pain of loss again.

He'd originally trained as a medic but after experiencing the horrors of war, he sought refuge in a fantasy world.

As a child, he'd loved the glitz and glamor Hollywood offered. After a brief stint in the war where he witnessed the deaths of friends, he found an escape from the harshness of reality returning to the fantasy of Hollywood

I wondered what sort of woman would be able to touch this frozen man at the deepest level. Everything in his life was controlled measured, predictably precise. I wondered what if the darkness of the past, his unhealed wounds began to impact his work, stifling his creativity and threatening to destroy everything he had fought so hard to achieve.

I wondered what if, as part of his recovery, he was forced to spend time with a woman so opposite in every way to the order he imposed in his life. And what if this woman was a children's art therapist. A woman unimpressed by the fame and fortune he'd amassed, but who believed strongly in the power of play, fun, and spontaneity—things he considered reckless

What if this woman had the power to transform his life, and he hers—but they were both afraid. Hearts have been broken, love lost, trust betrayed. What if this woman had her own wounds? Don't we all?

What would it take to make all the masks fall?

To be vulnerable? To risk it all? What would it take, in spite of the fear, to believe you deserve, you want, you need to give love a second chance?

You'll discover the answers in *Married by Christmas*. I hope you love this story as much as I loved writing it.

P.S. If you'd like to know more about these characters, inside peeks into the writing process, or be the first to know when a new book is released, subscribe to my newsletter here: http://eepurl.com/cigEsH. Please email me and I'll be in touch personally—I promise...mollie@molliemathews.com.

ACKNOWLEDGMENTS

I'm very blessed with some wonderful cheerleaders and writing friends. Instrumental in bringing Married by Christmas to life are Sandy Johnson, Rae Waterhouse, Bronwyn Sell, Laura Virgo, Pam Claughton, and Odile Boniface. Having your help made all the difference between finishing this book, and publishing it—or abandoning my dreams! Kimberly Reeland, your "Whooo wee's" spurred me on!

Coralie Urwin, I could not have polished this manuscript without you. Your responsiveness was amazing. And I loved that you enjoyed every moment of editing. It shows on every page.

Cate Walker, thank you again for being a very enthusiastic proof-reader. Your emails asking me when were you going to get the next chapters kept me on track.

And to the love of my life—Laurie Wills, my Templar Knight. Thank you for believing in me. Without your faith, support, commitment, inspiration, and love, I could never have written this book.

And Now

Thank you for purchasing and reading my books. You are more than my livelihood: you let me live my passion. Without your love of romance and belief in the power of love this book would never have been born. I really hope you loved this book as much as I enjoyed writing it. Here's to an extra-ordinary level of love and happiness in all our lives.

With love,

THANK YOU

Thank you for reading *Married by Christmas*... I hope you loved it. If you did...

1. Help other people find this book by writing a review
2. Signup for my new releases email to find out about the next book as soon as I release it, sign up here http://eepurl.com/ghM501
3. Email me at mollie@molliemathews.com with a copy of your honest review and let me know if you'd love to join my dream team and of advance readers
4. Follow me on BookBub, https://www.bookbub.com/authors/mollie-mathews

5. Stay in touch on Facebook, https://www.facebook.com/molliemathewsnz
6. Follow me on Twitter - https://twitter.com/Molliemathewsnz
7. Be inspired on Pinterest - https://nz.pinterest.com/molliemathews and Instagram - https://www.instagram.com/molliemathewsauthor
8. Follow my blog - https://molliemathews.wordpress.com

Keep reading for a preview of my next book in the *Passion Down Under* series, *Bride of Gold and* other passion-filled stories including *Flight of Passion* and *Claimed by The Sheikh* (available in paperback and eBook)

BRIDE OF GOLD

Book Two in the Passion Down Under series—
available now

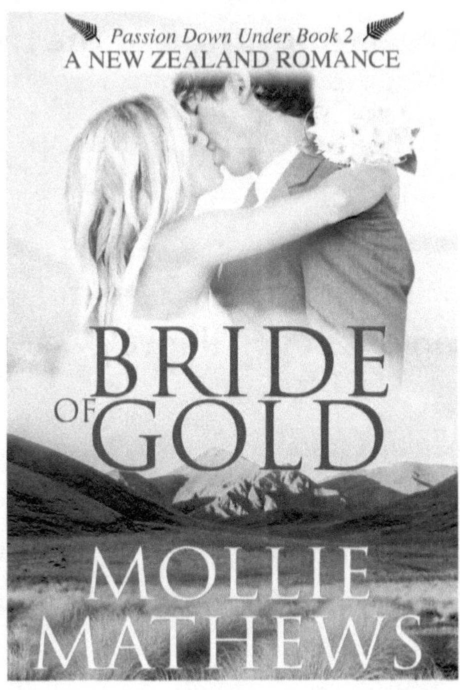

What if everything you believed was a lie?

When a lonely young American woman inherits a painting she discovers her whole life was a lie. Desperate for the truth, she goes in search of her true identity.The painting is her only clue. But everyone is determined to keep its secret past repressed, including Vitaliano Rossi, the Italian gold tycoon. Unnaturally suspicious of her motives, he wants the painting—and Alex—vanquished.

How can she discover who she really is and convince him that his love means more to her than gold?

Three women. Three lives. And the lies that bind them. Why is everyone afraid of the truth?

Set amongst the stunning backdrop of New Zealand's South Island.

If you love stories set in New Zealand, against a sensuous backdrop of art, you'll love *Bride of Gold*.

Praise for *Bride of Gold*

"The attraction between Vitali and Alex is electric and although the book is relatively clean, there is enough passion between them to boil water. As truths emerge and they come to an understanding of each other's motives, the love that has been simmering between them comes out in full force. I loved both Vitali and Alex and even though Vitali was arrogant and seemed to be self-serving, he is nevertheless an exciting hero, whilst Alex is the kind of woman we can all identify with. This is an excellent and somewhat suspenseful read."

~ Margaret Watkins

"I loved, loved, loved reading this book. What an absolute treat to read a book without skipping over scenes that are explicit and foul language! This is a very well-written story. Mollie really hit a winner with this one. I read it in two sittings because I could not put it down. The back and forth between Alexandra and Vitali had me chuckling and intrigued as to what the results were going to be. I will be reading more written by Mollie Mathews! I am drawn to anything New Zealand as it is on my bucket list."

~ Glenda

"I have a soft spot for New Zealand; it is one of the

most spectacular countries I have visited. Alex and Vitali have a connection on their first meeting, but not positive. They come to negotiate over a painting by Alex's dad. Their relationship continues with the ups and downs of incomplete communication of many couples. Still, their love grows despite all that is thrown their way. I really had trouble putting this book down to do stuff around the house that I needed to do. This is the first book I have read by this author and hope to read more."

~ Alethia

"Hard to set down! I very much enjoyed reading this book. The author had beautifully descriptive writing. I could easily picture the scenery she described from Gold Ridge Station and I would love to see if any areas in New Zealand match up to the picture in my head."

~ Amazon Review

"What a wonderful book this was.I just couldn't put it down, but had to read it at nights. How wonderful you have written this love story with so much passion and fighting for love and acknowledgment to get one to can give. Such wonderful loved-filled clean romantic books. Full of passion, love, and tenderness. Words can't describe the real way I found this book.Fantastic."

~ Istella van Rhyn

Book Two in the Passion Down Under series—available now

'You should never have responded to that email. I don't understand you, Alexandra.'

'Okay, so an email arrives out of the blue telling me the man who I thought was my father isn't, only my real father is dead and he's left me some valuable paintings—and I'm supposed to ignore that?'

'Why do you insist on digging up the past? I've told you no good will come of it.' Bitterness bled from her mother's words.

Alex Spencer pressed her lips together, momentarily fixing her gaze on the desolate New York sky as snow began to fall, before continuing to shovel summer clothes into a well-travelled leopard print suitcase.

They would never agree. She wanted to say, 'Mother, why are you making everything so difficult? Why won't you talk to me about him? Why did you never tell me the truth?' But she'd already asked and every time her mother evaded answering. Despite what her mother had done, for the sake of their tie of blood, which was the only thing left between them, she had to keep the peace.

'Why do you have to go back to New Zealand? What do you hope to achieve that you didn't six months ago? What point is there?' Elizabeth Spencer pressed, fixing disapproving eyes on her errant daughter.

'You know why I need to go back, Mother,' Alex said quietly, careful to stop exasperation creeping into her voice.

Her mother's blue eyes turned a chilly shade of grey. 'After all Charles and I have done for you. He's been more of a father to you than that man ever was.' The accusation whistled through her pursed lips. Why would you want to do something so selfish?

Alex forced herself to count to ten. It was as if her mother thought keeping something so important a secret from her own daughter all these years was no big deal. As though replacing a real dad with a surrogate father gave her a new identity.

How could Alex possibly explain without severing their relationship for good that finally she knew why she never felt understood, never felt accepted, never felt she belonged. That she could never find peace until she understood her past.

'I told you when I came back to New York for Christmas that I'd only be here for a few weeks. Please don't let us spend our last moments arguing.' Alex forced, an uncertain smile and didn't know if it would melt her mother's iciness. Why should she feel so guilty?

Her boutique travel business meant she was never home for long. She was like those dandelions; settling for a spell then blowing away. And she was no longer a child. Yet in this matter she longed for her mother's approval.

'Why can't you let go of this thing you've got about your father?' Her mother fired. 'What more do you have to know, for heaven's sake? He was an artist. He left you a painting. End of story.'

It wasn't the end of the story. It was far from it. In fact of the six paintings her biological father had left her in his will, one, she knew with gut-churning clarity, would unlock buried secrets. Secrets her mother seemed resolute never to divulge

'I want to know everything. I want to know about the man whose blood courses through my veins. I want to know why my hair is red. I want to know who I am and where I came from. Why can't you understand that?'

'There's nothing more to say. I was young. Impulsive. He was a mistake.'

Alex's stomach clenched. *She was a mistake.* Her mother didn't have to say it but her tone made it clear. She was the child nobody wanted.

Tension held Alex's body rigid as she continued packing. She had become skilled at masking her emotions: grief, loneliness, anger—especially anger. It flared inside her now but she held it in check. Up until six months ago Alex had known nothing of Ted Carr. If the email hadn't come from a solicitor in New Zealand notifying her of the unusual inheritance she would still think Charles Spencer was her real father.

The news had been devastating. She felt betrayed. Everything she thought was real—gone, her whole identity—a lie. At least now she knew why she had never felt loved. She was a painful reminder of a past everyone wished had never happened and they were determined to forget.

Alex gazed at her mother imploringly, hoping she'd explain. All she had to do was tell her about her past and Alex wouldn't be left to reassemble the shattered fragments of her identity alone. But Elizabeth turned her head briskly as though she couldn't bear to be confronted by the truth after all these years. She stared down at the heavy snow flurries blanketing the exclusive streets of Manhattan, freezing her daughter in a fortress of silence. Why was her mother so determined to keep everything about her past a secret?

'Alexandra, you're twenty-six years old for goodness' sake. Wandering the world like a gypsy, living in strange places as though you have no place to call home,' her mother complained, spinning around to face her daughter. 'You're just like your father,' she inadvertently let slip. She twisted her wedding ring between her fingers. 'It's just not normal. If you're not careful you'll wind up a lonely, old spinster.'

Alex flinched at her mother's criticism. 'I don't need a man,' she said solemnly, achingly aware of the hollowness of her tone. It was true. She didn't need a man—at least not the kind of men her mother constantly threw at her.

Elizabeth shook her head and heaved a defeated sigh. She marched to the bed and perched, her back rigid, on the steel-grey silk throw and glared at her headstrong daughter. 'Now there's a girl who made a good marriage,' she said tossing the December edition of Vanity Fair on the bed. "George's First Christmas" trumpeted the headlines beneath the chocolate box perfect family photo. 'When am I going to get some grandchildren?' her mother pouted.

'I'd rather be on my own than locked in a loveless marriage. I came close to that sentence—I won't be trying it again. Besides, you've told me yourself, where relationships are concerned I'm just one big failure.'

'Why do you keep dragging up the past?'

'Sometimes it's better not to run from the truth. Besides, let's face it, I don't have an A+ in relationships.'

'What are you looking for, Alexandra?' her mother asked tiredly. 'What do you want?'

I'd like to know that my father didn't abandon me. I need to know that I was loved. I want to feel good enough.' Alex's lips quivered and she forced a bright smile. 'I'll let you know when I find it.' Her voice dropped to a whisper as her thoughts trailed away, then, sensing her mother's impatient stare, plummeted back to the present. 'What I do know is that I don't want Jeremy Poot, or any of the other men you keep thrusting at me. I don't want to live the kind of life they'd want me to lead, trotting beside them like a show horse, a trophy to their careers.'

'You'd want for nothing.'

Alex bit her lip. Her mother was wrong. She'd tried going out with the sort of men her mother approved of and it didn't work. Devoid of passion, they cared more about their careers than their wives. And while her mother was prepared to settle for that, Alex never would. She wasn't after money and status; she still hoped for love.

To Elizabeth Spencer New York and its exclusive set of people was the only world worth knowing. Nothing could be better. But to Alex, the very notion of conforming to her wishes and masquerading in twin set and pearls, confined in a career as a high-society wife with zero autonomy was abhorrent. If there wasn't something better, then life wasn't worth living. She may as well be a vegetable, a cauliflower, for all the good it would do her.

Her gaze drifted out the window—the sky and streets a complete whiteout, masking everything that held any semblance of beauty.

'Oh, you're still here.' Charles Spencer's powerful frame dressed immaculately in a fine wool tuxedo filled the doorway. 'Come on Elizabeth,' he growled. 'We'll be late.'

Her mother hesitated then smiled tightly and rose to her feet.

'Don't worry, I'll make my own way to the airport.' Alex said, hoping her voice sounded sufficiently bright and nonchalant. She hadn't seriously thought she mattered enough to be taken to the airport. They would say their goodbyes here. Clearly she'd be doing everyone a favour. Out of sight, out of mind.

Ignoring Charles' disapproving glare she packed her Canon SLR and two extra lenses in her orange Photo Hatchpack, placed it in the suitcase and jammed layers of clothing around it for protection. They could get on with their lives and she could make peace with hers.

'You and that camera, and don't get me started on that leopard print suitcase! Can't you at least take something more respectable?' Elizabeth Spencer rolled her eyes as she crossed the room and stood dutifully at her husband's side.

'I'm not like you, Mother. I'm used to being different.'

In fact I'm nothing like you at all, Alex thought, glancing at her. The blonde strands of her mother's hair immaculately lacquered into a sleek bob, contrasted dramatically with her own unruly birds nest of jet-black curls. Her mother's tiny, slender figure was elegantly yet conservatively clothed to match her husband's. She was indeed the ultimate accessory to her husband's political ambitions—kilometres apart from Alex's generous curves hidden beneath layers of comfort. Her mother's skin looked untouched by the forty-five years of her life. No lines. No worry. No stress. She was capable of leaving that behind her, even when she was upset—unlike Alex who was continually criticized for being too sensitive and worried about everything.

But while they were worlds apart—and always would be—Alex could understand the drive that had taken her mother from poverty to become one of New York's top socialites. The determined, obsessive streak in her mother's nature was also in her own. Surely her mother realized that the more she kept the truth from Alex the more she needed to know.

'This is your home. Why can't you be happy here?'

Alex looked around the room, her gaze bouncing off the bleak white walls, then sweeping over the sterile glass and chrome designer pieces, and humorless white chintz drapes and bed linen. It had always felt like a museum to New York design than a home where she felt comfortable.

Perhaps as a child if, instead of telling her animals were too messy, she'd been allowed the luxury of the pet cat or dog she'd so desperately yearned for she might have felt less lonely. If, instead of being surrounded by kilometres of soulless concrete, she'd lived in a house where she could have had all sorts of pets, even chickens and horses, surrounded by space and nature, she would have felt more herself. Why was she so different? Why couldn't she be happy?

She looked up, fighting the sinking sensation in her stomach at the disappointment in her mother's eyes. 'I'm sorry,' she said. 'I'm really sorry I can't be the daughter you want. But what's right for you is not right for me. I have to create my own life.'

Elizabeth shook her head, 'I've tried so hard—and you can't say Charles hasn't been a good father. We've done everything we could for you.'

Alex's shoulders stiffened as Charles scowled in moody silence. He had always made her feel especially unwanted, shutting her out in a wall of disinterest, as though she never existed. 'Please don't think I'm not grateful.' Alex said quickly, feeling her mother's pain. 'It's just that—' She lifted her hands helplessly. It would be impossible to explain without sounding cruel. Despite everything her mother had done for her, every opportunity she had been given, how could she ever be happy knowing half of her DNA was a black void.

'Mother, you made your choices,' she said flatly. 'Let me make mine.'

A brooding disapproval settled on her mother's brow. 'He gave you up,' she shot bitterly. 'Then he throws a painting at you and you're all over him. What makes you think he wants you to know him now?'

Alex swallowed words of anger she knew would only harm, curling her fingers around the photo hidden in her pocket. The strange painting he had bequeathed to her held the key to the mystery. Alex was certain of it. Why else would he have left it to her?

'Why didn't he just disappear forever?' she

asked, careful to keep any hint of challenge from her voice.

'That's the point—he did disappear,' Charles said tersely. The blood vessel in his forehead pulsed as he braced his arms across his chest. 'Quite frankly the whole sordid affair is better dead and buried.'

Alex could well imagine how Ted Carr could have been frozen out of the marriage, left without a leg to balance on as far as custody was concerned. Or perhaps her father thought Alex was better off without him in her life. Undoubtedly Charles Spencer would have made that clear.

But Ted Carr hadn't forgotten his daughter. And Alex couldn't explain to her mother the strange affinity she now felt with him, even though he was no longer alive. The fact was that he'd left her something that was deeply meaningful to him. Hopefully by exhibiting the painting in New Zealand, someone somewhere might know what it meant.

'If you do this thing, Alexandra—well, I may as well never have had a daughter.'

'Please don't—please don't make me choose.'

'Hurry up, Elizabeth. We've done this thing to death. Let her go and make her own mistakes. Maybe then, like most women, she'll realize when she's onto a good thing,' Charles thundered.

'Well, it's clear you've made up your mind,

Alexandra,' her mother said turning to leave. 'You always were a willful child. Perhaps one day you'll realize your mother was right.'

As they bristled from the room without so much as a kiss or a hug Alex slumped on her bed and exhaled a bellyful of tension. Her temples pulsed, and her chest felt as though it had been twisted and squeezed like a tube of toothpaste. She flung her legs over the side of the bed and padded to the en-suite. She rattled through the drawer containing the three-dozen or so bottles of her most trusty essential oils and, selecting cinnamon, black pepper and lavender, dabbed several drops of each on a tissue. She inhaled the sweet empowering warmth of nature's magic elixir and glanced at her reflection in the mirror.

Who am I? Why am I the way I am? Why can't I settle? Staring back with dark rings under her eyes was a stranger, in a foreign body, in an environment that had never felt so alien. Were her dark chocolate eyes those of a man who broke her mother's heart, or a rake, a seducer, an uncaring man unable to keep his commitment? All she knew was she wasn't her anymore.

She had to return. She needed to know. Until then she could never be herself. Whoever she was. Maybe she would finally put her own ghosts to rest. Twin rivers of trepidation and the thrill of excitement surged through her. In less than 24 hours she would be 14369 kilometres closer to discovering who she really was and with this new understanding maybe life would get better.

It would be an adventure if nothing else. She had cast the dice and would live with how they fell.

Alex pressed against a pillar beneath the cavernous ceiling of the Auckland art gallery, suppressing a yawn as she fought a wave of jet lag. Clutching the exhibition catalogue to her chest she swept her gaze over the crowd gathered for the opening of the dazzling retrospective exhibition of her father's lifeworks. Only yesterday she had been in icy New York and now here she was in the heat of the New Zealand summer, surrounded by Veuve Clicquot, popping corks and intoxicating works of art. At the centre of the gallery stood Clive Gacos, the art dealer who had discovered the man she now knew was her father, exchanging air kisses and handshakes. Impeccably armoured in a steel-grey designer suit that complemented his trademark helmet of silver hair he looked in his element as he enthusiastically greeted a procession of collectors and socialites.

Alex crossed her arms protectively over her

chest as women flashed him far too-enthusiastic smiles, and fluttered acrylic nails in shallow waves. She hated crowds at the best of times and tonight, surrounded by so much pretence, she felt doubly out of her comfort zone. Nausea crawled through her stomach as she wondered if Clive's insistence she exhibit the painting had been one giant mistake. Would tonight flush out someone intimately connected to the powerful, yet haunting image? Someone who would help her unearth the past her mother and Charles wanted kept buried?

Her gaze drifted to the vast landscape her father had painted running the length of the far wall. "Lost Love". Two words that tore her heart apart. Looking at the painting now, she wondered if the name she'd given it still fitted. For some inexplicable reason, unlike all her father's other paintings, he'd left this one unnamed. Why did he leave so few clues to its meaning?

Barely conscious of the crowd pressing around her Alex's heart quickened as she scanned the craggy Southern Ranges, their soaring peaks troughed with a hurtle of blue and ochre and gold. Her gaze honed in on the hauntingly beautiful face of a woman, infused within the rocks. Why had her father painted a woman's face into the landscape? And whose was the face—so beautiful—yet so tragic?

The woman seemed to reach through time and space, lifting agonized eyes, calling Alex's name, drawing her deeper and deeper into the painting's mystery. Had something deeply personal happened to inspire the painting, something that could shed light on her past? For twenty-five years her life had been a lie. Months of searching for clues to her past had ended in granite walls of silence. Yet the way her heart pounded, and her eyes pooled with tears, and every hair on her body stood on end each time she looked at the painting, told her that there was a deeper reason her father wanted the painting to remain in her possession. Alex was sure her father was enticing her to discover the painting's secrets. Why else did he leave this particular painting in his will to the daughter he'd never met?

She tore herself away from "Lost Love" and stood at a distance observing people's reactions in the hope that she would discover someone who found the painting as meaningful as she did. An older woman stared at it the longest, her eyes pooling as she fingered the elaborate gold locket at her throat.

A young man and woman holding hands stopped in front of it, and the woman slipped her hand from her partner's as she stepped closer to study the face of the woman. A middle-aged man's body grew hard and tense as he looked, and he passed quickly by. Another man with a receding hairline flinched as if someone had punched him in the gut, and he reached a hand out to the painting, not quite touching the velvet plains of golden tussock and Rātā trees clinging fiercely to craggy rocks.

Dread wormed through her gut. The strange and enigmatic image evoked powerful reactions in them all, but none of them betrayed the fact they held the missing piece to her painful puzzle. She pressed her lips together, holding her face tight, as tears pricked her eyes.

Showing "Lost Love" was a hair-brained idea, like searching for a needle in a paddock of tussock. What real chance did she have of discovering someone who knew anything truly intimate about her dead father? Yet what else could she do? All her other enquiries had come to nothing.

Alex heaved a sigh of frustration and turned away. Clive Gacos caught her anxious gaze. His fluttering fingers flourished a greeting across the room as he slithered to her side. "Lost Love." I still think the title's a bit morbid.' He cocked his head to one side as his gaze darted from the catalogue to the painting before resting on Alex. 'Couldn't you have come up with something more commercial?'

Alex wanted to cry out "it's how I feel."

'You may be right, Mr Gacos,' she said, painting a mask of detached aloofness on her face. Instinct told her Clive was only interested in his fame and glory. Not her own painful story. She took his outstretched hand and felt a shiver snake through her spine as cold, hard, steely fingers shook hers.

'It's a fabulous turnout, my dear. I'm absolutely delighted.' Bleached white teeth flashed a self-satisfied smile.

'Are you sure that this is the best way to unearth someone who may know something about this painting, Mr Gacos? You know how firmly my father was against it being exhibited.'

'"Field of Dreams" or "Secret Passion" would have been a better name. Like a book the right title can boost sales,' he said glancing at the painting 'That's interesting', Alex said flatly. 'But "Lost Love" is not for sale.'

Eerie, pale eyes looked right through her. 'My dear, everything is for sale.'

'No, Mr Gacos. It's not. I'm looking for answers. A sale won't achieve that.' Had she been wrong to trust him? 'Besides you told me yourself, my father made it quite clear that the painting must never leave my possession.'

'My dear, 40 years in the industry has taught me one thing, what an artist says and what an artist means are quite, quite different things. If you gave me ten dollars for every time I've heard, 'This is my favorite work, I'll never part with it,' or some other nonsense I'd be a hundred-fold richer.' His reptilian eyes scanned her face as though searching for a weakness in her resolve. 'Of course none of this matters now that your father is dead.'

Dead. Alex's eyes misted as the finality of the word hit her unexpectedly. It was ridiculous. Eleven months ago she hadn't even known geologist, turned painter, Ted Carr, known in art circles as Jimmie Goldie, was her father and since then she'd had plenty of time to accept the fact that he was gone. But she couldn't help feeling regret. If only she'd known her father. If only he was by her side now. Although in a strange way he was, she mused, her eyes misting as she gazed at the painting. Infused with his energy, his passion, his spirit "Lost Love" was her only link. It was as though the painting was his voice—allowing him to speak through time and space. But only to those with ears who could hear and Alex still had no idea what he was saying. Maybe she was reading too much into it. Maybe it was just a painting. But why did her father want her to have it?

'I expect this exhibition to arouse even more interest, and the longer we hold off the more the painting will appreciate in value.' Clive blabbered on, oblivious of her raw grief.

Alex clenched her teeth, shutting back a retort at his thoughtless remark. This wasn't the time to be emotional, nor to incite conflict. She hated disharmony and discord. And although she'd been continually teased because she always chose the peaceful route, putting him in his place would only get him off side.

'Remind me again, Mr Gacos, just how well did you know my father?' she said gently.

'I told you, I discovered him. Made him a sell-out success.'

'Yes, but what was he really like?'

'Oh, I don't know. We never met.'

'But you were his dealer?'

'I deal in works of art, Miss Spencer. Not people. Your father liked his privacy. I respected that.'

'Didn't you wonder why he hid his true identity?'

'My dear, you know half the celebrities in the world use fake, made-up names. Careers live and die by people's memorability. It's all part of the game. Do you really think Andy Warhol's paintings would sell for astronomical sums if he called himself Andrew Warhola? Your father was smart. Jimmie Goldie, or Ted Carr—ask yourself, who's the better investment?'

Tension knotted her shoulders. She was getting nowhere.

'Want some advice?'

No.

'Take it from me. There's no mystery—just a finely executed brand strategy. And you, the lucky beneficiary. So what, he left you this painting. Maybe his conscience got the better of him. In my opinion it's an exceptional piece of work, one of his finest, and tantalizingly one that the art world has never seen before. If I were you, I'd sell it. Realize the cash. Return to New York. Go live your life.'

Go live your life. She would—but not before she had her answers. Alex's gaze drifted back to the crowd. Her only hope was that someone would reveal something in their reaction to the painting. Surely if anyone was connected intimately it would hit them with the same power-punch to the gut as it did her every time she looked at it.

Suddenly she was distracted by a blaze of rustic color. The most ridiculously handsome man Alex had ever seen strode toward her. His six-foot frame wore an immaculately tailored camel jacket, cut from the finest Merino wool and fashionably faded jeans gracing a powerful physique.

His skin was deeply tanned, his hair glossy black —wavy and slightly tousled. Not a classically handsome pasty metro-sexual like the English suitors her mother continually threw in her path. But a ruggedly handsome man, who looked as though he would be equally at home in a New York boardroom dressed in a sleek Armani suit as he would be rustling cattle in a tough New Zealand Swandri. The man oozed passion, purpose—and danger.

She watched entranced as his gaze swept the room, standing rigidly in the archway with a presence that emanated command. He had a strong, arresting face, coldly handsome with no lines of weakness. A disturbingly primitive tug of attraction quaked through her body. She could imagine this man commanding a Roman Legion, or leading a charge of Templar Knights. He oozed the power of a man who made his own rules, ruthlessly sweeping aside anyone who stood in opposition. A smile fluttered to her lips as she imagined the shock on her mother's face if she came home with a man so raw and rugged. To her discomfort she found the idea thrilling and quickly sanctioned her recklessness.

Whether the Adonis had read her mind Alex had no idea, but as he carved his way through the crowded gallery he slowed his stride. He paused opposite her and looked at her with the level unwavering gaze of a ravenous lion. Her heart raced. Near them people glided around the paintings, the vacuous height of the vaulted gallery ceiling amplifying peoples voices, but she was trapped with him in exploding silence.

Usually she dismissed such attention. But this was more than a fleeting appraisal of desirability, more than an appreciation of the curvaceous femininity of her figure. It was an arrogant assessment projecting the confident knowledge that he could have her if he wanted. The only question appeared to be would she be worth the effort?

A frisson of danger scuttled down Alex's spine. Under his penetrating gaze Alex felt like a naked model posing for a ravenous sculptor. She picked at the black sequins of her dress, immediately regretting wearing the figure-hugging cocktail number she'd purchased for the formal opening night.

She never dressed up ordinarily, and hated wearing black, but she had wanted to blend in with the art-gallery noir that she knew everyone else would be wearing. It was the only suitable dress she'd found at the second hand store on Queen Street in the few hours she had to spare since arriving in Auckland and the only dress that came anywhere close to fitting. She cursed the shimmering sequins for attracting his attention, as her face flared with humiliating heat.

His piercing green eyes rested for long, uneasy moments on Alex's quivering lips. His lips curved sardonically as his gaze inched with leisurely thoroughness before dropping to where her dress clung to her breasts.

Every whisper of hair on her body stood like sentries armed for defence. Yet to her intense humiliation she found her barriers weakened. Was that pleasure? Longing? Desire she felt flood her body with warmth. She couldn't be sure. It had been years since she'd been touched. Certainly, never by anyone so virile. For the briefest moment she found herself wondering what it would be like to be taken by such a man. Every remnant of her rational mind fought the dangerous feeling, but the more she struggled the more her body betrayed her.

Suddenly, with an air of explosive tension the weight of the stranger lurched forward. His face spun away from her. Alex followed the direction of his fixed gaze, piqued that his interest in her had been so totally diverted. She couldn't see his expression but she could sense his undiluted fury.

In the next instant he propelled himself forward through the crowd, a dozen lithe strides bringing him within a foot of "Lost Love".

Her pulse rate ricocheted as she realized with a jolt he was staring at "Lost Love". She watched transfixed as the stranger froze as if in shock. Then shook his head in disbelief. After several tense moments he riffled through the catalogue he carried. His shoulders tensed as he read the small caption, then scrutinised the painting again. He thrust his arms out as if to wrench the painting from the wall. His hand tightened into a closed fist crumpling the catalogue and thrusting it into his pocket.

Alex's heart pounded then took a dive as her

mind raced ahead, struggling to understand the intensity of his reaction. Could he be the man who could unravel her mysterious past?

He swung around, his face set in determined purpose, his gaze scanning quickly over the people in the room. They passed over Alex without a flicker of recognition, every muscle of his face taunt with savagery.

'Who is he?'

'I don't know, but he looks important.' Clive said in a low voice. 'Let me handle this.'

Clive was off and moving with the silent speed of a cobra toward the stranger before Alex could object. Tension jack-knifed through her chest. What should she do? Run after Clive and risk getting in the way? The stranger had dismissed any interest in her with the aloof detachment of a man who would never cede control. Instinct told her where she was concerned he was untameable and, like a wild wolf, the wrong move would send him running. Besides, Clive's reputation for netting the elusive was legendary.

She reached for a glass of champagne from a passing waitress and took tiny gulps as she hovered anxiously. Would Clive find out what had incited such a powerful reaction? Would the stranger reveal why he had responded so strongly? Perhaps the painting incited something deep within his soul? Impossible.

The man did not appear to have a soul or he would not have dismissed her so coolly. Her heart pulsed with the sting of his rejection. He was clearly a collector like many others in the gallery. A numbers man who no doubt prided himself on his many conquests and the number of artworks he possessed.

Alex gripped the stem of the glass as she watched the scene unfold. As Clive tried to beguile him with his charming smile the stranger's shoulders tensed. Fear rumbled through her as cataclysmic as an earthquake. Was Clive failing? She cursed herself for allowing him to take the lead.

A woman with a beehive hairdo, her long neck over-saturated with Opium perfume paused in front of her obstructing her view.

'Excuse me,' Alex said, inhaling a heady mix of cinnamon and spice, as she pressed past the woman. The stranger was no longer in front of the painting. Where had he gone? Her heart hammered as she stood on her tiptoes and scoured the room.

A slice of golden caramel moving like a bullet caught her eye as the stranger strode toward the exit.

Like the sun setting over the ranges in "Lost Love", in a blink he was gone.

'Goodbye,' she whispered, consumed again by the sea of black.

A heavy blanket of heat enveloped her. Now what? She yawned as a wave of tiredness weighed upon her. Jet lag still catching up on her, she thought, as she glanced at her watch and mentally calculated the time difference between New York and New Zealand. Tenacious to a fault she had no doubt Clive Gacos would try again to hook the stranger. She could pick his brains tomorrow when she was better rested. It was probably pointless to hang around the gallery anyway, fantasising possibilities from people's reactions to "Lost Love". She had to do something more constructive. But tonight, she thought happily, had been a very, very good start. Someone in the room tonight held the key. The door it opened would forever change her life.

~

Did you enjoy this excerpt?
BRIDE OF GOLD

Book Two in the Passion Down Under series—available now from Amazon here: getBook.at/BrideofGold

EXCERPT: FLIGHT OF PASSION

FLIGHT OF PASSION

BOOK ONE IN THE TRUE LOVE SERIES AVAILABLE NOW

Past love and the obsessions that bind them.

Devastatingly handsome Oliver Hart is used to getting what he wants. Single, thirty-five and a committed bachelor, he plays by his own rules. On a personal quest to catch a rare, elusive and very valuable butterfly, he's unwittingly distracted by a former flame, Ruby Diaz—a woman who callously abandoned him eight years earlier.

Deciding he wants to reclaim the beauty as his own, in his mind, it's as good as done.

But Ruby is not his for the taking. Promised to the son of a wealthy landowner, she refuses to succumb to his charms. On a quest to save her family's land, Ruby knows she must put duty first, and silence the passionate stirrings of her heart. But Oliver doesn't make things easy for her. He's not taking no for an answer.

Risking everything to help the woman he loves to gain her freedom, Oliver entangles himself in an emotional net that alters his life forever. Sacrificing his own selfish pursuit to help Ruby, he realizes that you may be able to own something, but you can never own someone—especially the women you love.

Have you ever wanted to be with someone who sent your heart soaring but threatens your sense of security? Someone who lifts you clear out of the water, but you're not sure will be around to catch you when you fall head over heels in love? Flight of Passion is a rapturous tale of beauty, obsession and the transformational power of unconditional love.

PRAISE FOR FLIGHT OF PASSION

"This is a well written book that tantalizes your senses. Will Oliver be able to convince Ruby that she loves him enough to disobey her family? Can they find each other when all seems lost? An excellent book that I highly recommend. It will have you laughing with joy and crying with sadness."

~ Marie Fraser

"Mollie Mathews has written a beautifully scripted story of two people wildly attracted to each other, but too constrained by family expectations to allow themselves to commit. When they meet again after eight years can they move beyond old patterns of behavior or are they doomed to always want, but never have?"

~ Jane Whitmeyer

"This book is a carefully crafted, truly original story. Mollie's wonderfully descriptive narrative paints a picture in which it is easy to lose oneself—I really felt like I had been to Mexico by the time I had finished. Her butterfly theme echoes throughout the book both literally and figuratively. The main characters, Oliver and Ruby, are each conflicted in their own ways. Despite facing challenges, both ultimately find the strength to work through their difficulties to emerge better people, and most importantly, triumph over adversity together. A touching and heart-warming book, well worth a read."

~ Cathy Rioran

"Fast paced, heart wrenching, completely unexpected twists, excellent storyline, and a hell of a good read. You just gotta love Mollie's imagination and expertise in her writing."

~ Rae Waterhouse

"I fell in love with Ruby and Oliver, they are so good for each other, but both are so filled with garbage that their families filled them with, that they can't see what's in front of them. And when they finally realize that diamonds don't have a hold to what they had, they are about to lose it. The butterflies remind me of how ethereal life is and it is up to us to not waste it, but live the fullest and best we can."

~ **Advance reviewer**

"I really enjoyed Flight of Passion! I loved the descriptions of the butterflies and of the setting of the farm in Mexico. Wonderfully descriptive writing that transports you to a golden orchard filled with butterflies. Perfect for a cold winter's evening curled up by the fire."

~ **Linda Buckhingham**

PROLOGUE

G ROWING UP OLIVER WAS LEFT WITH THE impression he wasn't worthy. First by his parents who at the age of four sent him to the bottom of the world. It was as if they didn't know what to do with their infinitely curious and energetic child. It was as if sending him to the most prestigious boarding school in New Zealand absolved them of their responsibility, the responsibility which was every parents—or should be, he thought bitterly—to love their child unconditionally.

After his run in with a box of matches they told him he would amount to nothing. He proved them wrong. At sixteen he left New Zealand and headed for New York. It was true. If he could make it there he could make it anywhere. With the ruthless determination he was both admired and feared for like King Kong on steroids he quickly climbed to the top of the property acquisition tree.

He was king of the beasts, the man everyone wanted at their dreary New York parties, full of checkbook philanthropists who would never stoop to get close to the people their showy donations benefitted. Parties, like the one where he'd first met Ruby Diaz

Ruby had fluttered into his life like a breath of fresh air. She had lit up the room with her illuminating presence and dazzlingly rare beauty, not just on the outside, but the inside too. Her authenticity had the scent of violets—too guileless for pretense.

His darling Ruby. Oliver swallowed hard, refusing to succumb to the wave of angry hurt that swum from his heart to his throat.

For three blissful years they were inseparable. But no matter how much success he acquired, how extraordinarily wealthy he became, he wasn't good enough for the Diaz's darling Ruby. He never knew why she flew from his life, disappearing as quickly as she'd arrived. She had said nothing, given him no explanation, not even the courtesy of a call.

The Diaz family and the way Ruby had callously abandoned him reminded Oliver he would never be worthy—he was unlovable. Perhaps he should thank them for sparing him further hurt. Thanks to them and his hopeless parents he swore never to love again.

And that suited him just fine.

OBSESSION

I would like to be the air that inhabits you

~ Margaret Atwood ~

1

WOULD SELLING *BUTTERFLY LOVERS* REALLY free him of painful memories he'd rather forget?

Common sense told Oliver Hart that *Butterfly Lovers* was just a painting. An inanimate object, incapable of controlling him. But that was the trouble —it did control him, seducing him with its beauty, twisting his heart with bittersweet memories.

He'd intended to keep it . . . her . . . forever. His heartbeat seemed to almost stop as he thought of Ruby Diaz, the woman who had inspired the painting's commission. He rubbed his powerful chest, trying to ease the painful tightness that constricted his lungs as he surveyed the crowd gathered for the charity art auction.

It was time to let them both go. But would he ever be free?

His gaze swept over the minimalist, exquisitely designed interior, lingering over the priceless abstract by Rothko adorning a charcoal-black wall, at Hillcrest, his newly acquired mansion, and New Jersey's most expensive country estate.

Tonight, though, it was *Butterfly Lovers* which held in its grip women dripping with diamonds, and men clad in Armani. Locked in shared awe, they clustered around the painting, studying every line, every pulsating color.

Oliver wondered if their eyes ached as his did with a heady mix of pleasure and pain just to stand in its spellbinding presence. Or were they trying to decode the painting's hidden secrets?

Like a moth to a seductive flame, his eyes drifted to the bottom of the painting. Nobody, but one other person, would ever be able to decipher the graffiti-styled line of poetry scrawled in throbbing orange along the bottom of the painting.

Painful memories bled into his consciousness. Why the hell couldn't he shake her?

Butterfly Lovers. The painting was aptly named, he mused forcing his mind from the woman who had inspired the purchase. The dancing kaleidoscope of color reminded Oliver of his collection of exotic butterflies—his hobbyhorse and quiet obsession.

Dazzling sapphire blues, glistening watermelon pinks, pulsating canary yellows with shimmering oranges—flew from the canvas, and ricocheted off the marble floor which had been polished to a mirror-like gleam.

He had commissioned the painting in a move of uncharacteristic impulsiveness eight years earlier when he was 22 and madly in lust with Ruby. A 20 year-old exotic beauty, she'd fluttered into his life, bringing with her eternal sunshine, and air so fresh it seeped through the iron fortress he'd built around his heart.

Butterfly Lovers encapsulated the vitality, optimism and positivity she exuded. It was a rare piece which the serious art connoisseurs who gathered here this evening would die to possess. Oliver's brow furrowed, aware many were drawn here not by the desire to possess the contemporary art world's finest paintings, but insatiable voyeurs hungry to glimpse the inner world of one of America's wealthiest and most elusive bachelors.

Immensely private, he'd never opened any of his palatial homes to the public before. Not homes, *houses*, he corrected. He congratulated himself as he glanced around the clinical, museum-like surroundings. The dark walls and sophisticated lighting, spotlighting priceless works of art, created a sophisticated, yet austere, facade. If a building was truly a reflection of its owner, as many designers believed, the interior aptly reinforced the stereotypes perpetuated in the media—moody, dark, mysterious and strictly hands-off.

There was some truth to that, but it was not the whole truth.

Oliver's eyes drifted to the spiraling staircase and the heavy gold braided rope barricading the entrance to the upper level. He never let anyone get beyond the ground floor of his psyche. Some tried, but few persevered. No one, other than Ruby had ever penetrated his fortified armor. And that was a mistake.

He was complicated.

No doubt someone here tonight would go home and tweet that he was something of a social outcast, and arrogant to boot, Oliver thought as he hovered in the background. The fact was that he preferred his own company to engaging with his guests—predominantly wealthy financiers and bankers.

He knew his contempt was hypocritical, given he didn't care who reached into their pockets. But there was something decidedly unpalatable about bankers and the merciless way they preyed on the vulnerable. Tonight, he would gladly encourage them to part with their millions.

As he glanced at his reflection in the floor length window it struck him how far he had come from the days when just finding money to support himself and his little sister had been a struggle. Resplendent in an immaculately tailored Dolce & Gabbana tuxedo cut from the finest Italian wool, he looked like he belonged.

Oliver rubbed his hand over his pecs, powerfully aware of the Maori-inspired tattoo coiled over his shoulder that the crisp white linen of his shirt concealed. His hands pulsed with renewed conviction. It was his touchstone—a symbolic reminder that he was fierce and untouchable—a warrior businessman and an impenetrable lover.

On a good day, he even fooled himself.

But no matter how easy it was to make millions, no matter how many things he acquired, he'd never found a sense of contentment.

Except with—

Oliver bit down on his teeth, grinding them together in a futile attempt to crush memories he was determined not to revisit.

He glanced at his Rolex. 7:03:02. Irritability coursed through his veins. What the hell was the auctioneer waiting for? He fixed him with a piercing look, firing his unspoken annoyance through the crowd.

Tardiness was something he abhorred, and doubly-so tonight, he thought as he locked on the important call he had to make. In one hour it would be 8am in New Zealand and his sister, as punctual as he was, would be anxiously waiting.

As though feeling the pointed tip of Oliver's anger the auctioneer looked up. His relaxed smile quickly shattered as he was forced to confront the aggressive glint in Oliver's eyes, the rigid set of his shoulders, the brutally hard line of his jaw.

The auctioneer banged his hardwood gavel on the sounding block with short urgent thuds, his florid face ballooning as the chatter continued.

"Ladies and gentlemen, can I have your attention?" More insistent hammering. "Attention! Attention!"

The chatter fell to an orderly whisper, extinguished finally by the auctioneer's solemn voice.

"As you know, tonight is a unique opportunity to savor the extraordinary passions of Oliver Hart. Renowned as an astute business man, Oliver Hart is also an obsessive collector," he said.

"He has one of the most significant collations of contemporary art in the world. Not only a man of significant wealth, Oliver Hart, founder of Hart Luxury Hotel Consortium, is a man of outstanding generosity. All the funds raised by tonight's art auction will provide relief for those affected by last month's devastating earthquake in New Zealand, where he spent much of his childhood."

Oliver studied his feet as a thunder of applause quaked through the room, amplifying as it echoed off the walls.

Childhood.

The word was like a vicious punch to his stomach. Oppressive memories pounded his brain, and this time there was no silencing them.

Suddenly he was four years old again. Four years old and frightened. Lonely. Abandoned. Trapped in a jungle of strangers. Abandoned by bickering parents into a boarding school, neither one willing to let the other have custody. Selfishly caring more about winning against each other than the needs of their own child. And then there was his father.

His jaw locked as he bit down hard, swallowing a toxic cocktail of grief and anger. The brutal beatings hadn't hurt nearly as much as the verbal abuse and discouragement he'd suffered when he told them he wanted to be like his grandfather and study butterflies. The abuse had only intensified when he turned his back on the legal career his father had wanted. *'You'll never achieve anything. I wish you'd never been born. How dare you defy me you worthless piece of shit,'* the pain of these beatings had long healed—but those words still hurt.

Freezing sweat clung to Oliver's body in a vice-like grip, as he recalled the scorn his father rained upon him during his few personal visits. He paced across to the open window, inhaling deeply as he struggled to rip himself free from the shards of the past. Jesus, what sort of father tries to have his son institutionalized?

To some, it might seem ironic that he should be so generous to a country where he spent such an unhappy childhood, but Oliver didn't like to think of others suffering.

He forced his mind back to the present.

"Tonight's opening painting *Butterfly Lovers* is a significant artwork," the auctioneer continued, glancing down at his notes.

Oliver didn't have to read his words to know that what he would reveal was a shallow rendition of the truth. Only two people in the world truly knew just what *Butterfly Lovers* meant.

He glanced around the room thinking Ruby might have come, hoping with all his willpower she hadn't.

2

HE FORCED HIMSELF NOT TO BETRAY THE turmoil of emotions jack-knifing through his body as the massive painting was carried to the makeshift podium.

The butterfly theme had held so much promise. He'd never really bought into Ruby's tales about the transformative power of art to heal. But back then privately he'd hoped her optimism might rub off. With her by his side, and by owning the painting, perhaps he could shed a skin, free himself of his deformed past, re-emerge in a new skin. Undamaged. Someone nearing perfection. A better man. The sort of man Ruby deserved.

He'd been a fool.

Oliver's spine stiffened. He'd intended to keep it

. . .

her . . . forever. But even good intentions couldn't make up for a lifetime's inability to commit. He moved towards the terrace, widening the distance between him and the painting. He would no longer succumb to the painting's potent power to remind him of his failings.

"Created specifically for Oliver over seven years ago by struggling contemporary artist CG Tombly—only Oliver could have foreseen its financial potential."

Oliver's brow furrowed. The suggestion he had acquired the painting for commercial gain, rankled him. If he wasn't such a private man he might have told the crowd the truth. He'd made the mistake of talking candidly once before—a mistake he wouldn't be making again.

In its place he'd created a new habit—a habit of keeping his emotional life to himself, one he wasn't about to break. Soon the painting, and the painful memories of the only woman capable of making him feel, would be shed and he could devote himself to less painful obsessions.

"As always, Oliver's timing is impeccable. The painting's value has rocketed in the same soaring capacity as the palatial hotel Oliver's company has recently constructed in Dubai–so high it almost touches the gods."

The auctioneer flung his hands into the air to

accentuate his point. "Oliver Hart," he said, nodding in his direction and pointing to his towering 6-foot, 2-inch frame, "never does anything small."

Oliver thrust his hands in his pockets and glanced out the window refusing to look at the painting as the bidding began.

In a few fist-clenching minutes it would all be over and he could get on with his life.

His gaze drifted to the sculpture garden, lying beyond the pool, alighting on a solitary bronze sculpture by Brancusi. The modernist interpretation of Hercules holding the world on his shoulders, with its roughly hewn egg shaped sphere symbolizing earth had always appealed to him.

Balanced precariously on a towering sculpted wood base, the odd shape and the large crater severing the middle of the sphere challenged conventional notions of perfection and reminded him of humanity's rawness.

As his gaze lingered over the sculpture it occurred to him that repairing his scars, so deep that no relationship he started ever endured, required a Herculean effort.

No wonder the painting had failed.

But he still wanted to believe, as the ancient Greeks had, that art had a powerful ability to transform lives. He only hoped that selling the painting finally fulfilled this purpose. Perhaps then the painful memories that still haunted him could be turned to good.

He turned and fixed his gaze upon the audience. Who would be its new owner he wondered as the opening bid of one million was made. Would it go to Don Hermes, the impotent pharmaceutical giant, standing just ahead of him, or some other equally innocuous purchaser? Or would some anonymous bidder calling from China, Europe or the Middle East be the lucky buyer?

"$12 million? Do I have $12 million?" The bags under the auctioneer's eyes shifted as he tilted his head forward, and peered under his glasses.

"A small price to pay," he continued, his gaze briefly flickering to Oliver, "for a painting personally commissioned by a man who defies every category and transcends every cliché: a man with tremendous gusto and creative generosity."

The auctioneer's eyes flew to a scantily dressed blonde hovering hopefully next to Oliver. "A man who has yet to be pinned down."

Oliver caste her a dismissive look and moved further toward the back of the room.

"$12 million we have," cried the auctioneer's assistant, nodding vigorously as he pressed his iPhone firmly to his ear.

Oliver's heart lurched as the bidding began.

"$13 million," the assistant taking telephone bids shouted, raising his hand.

"$13.2 million." The auctioneer's eyes darted between the phone bidder and two men determined to claim the painting as their own.

Explosive tension hovered as one of the two remaining bidders turned their attention away.

"$13.5 million! At $13.5 million the painting will be sold," the auctioneer warned. He suspended the gavel in the air, pausing as he scanned the room.

"$17.4 million," came a guttural, low growl from the front of the crowd.

A record price!

The room fell silent under the weight of the bid, then buzzed with irritatingly discordant voices, their murmurs of awe and envy a rising tide of white noise.

Oliver's eyes darted to the front row. Over $14 million? The price was ridiculous. Someone must want it desperately. But who and why?

He was acquainted with the deep pockets of unbridled obsession. He understood intimately the seductive power of the painting.

But this was crazy bidding.

There had to be a compelling reason surpassing the usual appreciation of an art-lover. At that price it could hardly be an investment buy.

So that left . . . what?

Oliver paced the back of the room in agitation unable to see the face of the man who had placed this latest bid. He caught a glimpse of the woman next to the anonymous bidder as she shook a sexy spill of sun-kissed curls down her back. The familiar gesture sent shockwaves to his heart.

It couldn't be.

Her head turned slightly.

Oliver stood still, as if immobile, as if turned to stone.

Ruby Diaz.

His Ruby.

3

———————

A SYMPHONY OF EMOTIONS CRASHED through his veins as he saw a possessive arm snake around Ruby's waist and realized with horror the identity of the serpent she was with. Oliver threw back his shoulders, his muscular jaw tilted forward in defiance as he looked at the nauseatingly familiar figure.

Carlos Torres, the New York based, Mexican banking magnate and the-soon-to-be owner of *Butterfly Lovers.*

He could not let his painting—their painting— fall into her lover's clutches—a man as unscrupulous as he was deceptively charming.

Oliver's overactive mind raced with scenarios. He could draw from his own accounts the money for the earthquake fund—adding to the millions he had already donated.

But he knew with chilling certainty he was powerless to flout protocol, to bend the rules, to manipulate the outcome to suit his own desires. He knew only too well that once the auction had started, *Butterfly Lovers* could not be withdrawn.

"At this price, we'll sell," the auctioneer's eyes swept the room for any last bids.

The muscles in Oliver's chest tightened as he saw the auctioneer's gavel ascend into the air.

He watched helplessly as Carlos pulled Ruby toward him and folded her into his arms. The bitter taste of jealousy flooded his mouth.

The gavel sank toward the sounding block with freeze-frame inevitability. A splintering crack as wood met wood confirmed it was over with chilling clarity.

Oliver's hand tightened into a closed fist, crumpling the *Butterfly Lovers* catalogue into obscurity.

His heart rate pulsated making his chest feel as though it was about to implode, as Ruby turned and he watched with shock the way she wilted under Carlos' dominant presence, the light of passion missing from her eyes. She seemed sad and vulnerable—and the Ruby he knew was neither.

Something was wrong.

His rational mind thundered a warning. Don't get involved.

What business was it of his if she wanted to make a life with that snake? None. Not ordinarily. But Ruby wasn't ordinary. Accepting and accommodating maybe, but something told him there was more to their union than met the eye.

He clenched his fists and cursed softly fighting against the impulse to save her from a big mistake. Playing rescuer would invite complications he didn't need.

Especially now.

What he needed was a distraction. What he needed was uncomplicated sex—not to reignite an obsession. Ruby had already proven herself capable of breaking his heart mercilessly.

Not so with paintings and sculptures and his beloved butterflies, he mused, forcing his thoughts back to his collections. Once possessed they would never leave without his consent. And he could never make them cry. His jaw clenched as bitter memories of his parents' feuding pounded in his ears. His mother's heart-wrenching cries once heard, never forgotten.

He must not be distracted. He must not allow Ruby to get close. Obviously she had engineered Carlos to buy the painting, knowing full well how it would torture Oliver. She tortured him all those years ago and it was clear she intended to continue the onslaught. She could have that damned painting, he mused as unwelcome, undesired, uncontrollable passions, long forgotten but now unbridled, threatened to escape.

He rested one shoulder against the floor length window, his attention locked on Ruby as she freed herself from Carlos' clutches and fluttered through the swelling crowd toward the patio.

She possessed an innate and natural elegance that caused his glands to salivate, wetting his appetite in open defiance of his will. Her legs screamed danger—their long, slender length accented in scorchingly sharp stilettos that threatened to kill.

Kill his resolve. Kill his self-control. Kill him all over again.

He reached for a glass of whiskey from a passing waitress. He rocked the glass from side to side and studied the rough ice-chunks crashing through the amber liquid, then knocked the drink back, drowning his conflicting emotions.

Like a moth drawn to light he savored the way her floor length, silk dress clung to her lithe figure, her hibiscus red dress shimmering under the halogen lights like the wings of a newly emerged butterfly.

The way the vibrant color of her dress contrasted so deliciously with the flock of black cocktail dresses and designer dark suits everyone else favored brought a smile to his lips. Ruby had always stood out from the crowd.

Walk away, stay away. The voice in his head pitched high and shrill like an ambulance siren, as he fought an instinctive need to free her from a bad mistake.

The irregularly cut crystal pressed into his fingers as he gripped the glass. His life had rapidly become complicated.

He craned his neck as he momentarily lost sight of her, searching over the sea of heads and glittering diamonds.

Like the shards of ice in his glass, his hardened intention to stay detached was fracturing.

Plastering on a face of extreme nonchalance, he pushed determinedly towards her through the crowd as she stepped onto the patio and gazed forlornly up at the stars.

Why the hell was she with a dickhead like Carlos.

Glancing at his watch, Oliver wondered if he could find out what he needed to know in less than 20 minutes?

DID YOU ENJOY READING THIS EXCERPT?...

Thank you for purchasing and reading my books. You are more than my livelihood—you let me live my passion. Without your love of romance and belief in the power of love, this book would never have been born. I really hope you loved this excerpt from my full-length novel *Flight of Passion* as much as I enjoyed writing it.

Purchase the full-length copy and discover what happens next.

Flight of Passion: Book One in the True Love series available now from all good bookstores

Flight of Passion: Book One in the True Love series available now from all good bookstores

Here's to an extra-ordinary level of love and happiness in all our lives.

With love,

OUT NOW...CLAIMED BY THE SHEIKH

BOOK TWO IN THE TRUE LOVE SERIES

The secret she kept from the Sheikh...

A grief-stricken Sheikh Tariq na Hassir, the formidable ruler of the Kingdom of Avana, arrives in Paris to claim his brother's child after a car crash killed his parents--unaware that the child isn't their biological son. Salim is Tariq's son, with his former lover, a renowned architect.

Three years ago, after being banished by Tariq from his desert kingdom, Melanie Jones secretly gave her baby to Tariq's childless brother and his wife, in a swap the world was never supposed to know about.

The tragedy pulls her back to the world that rejected her and the man who abandoned her--the only man capable of turning her carefully controlled world upside down.

Tariq will do whatever it takes to protect his legacy, including claiming Melanie as his bride and his son as heir before scandals ensue.

But Melanie has other plans for her future—a westernized life where she's free to operate her own business and control her own life.

If you love true romance and beautiful love stories, set against a sensuous backdrop of the desert, art, and architecture you'll love *Claimed by The Sheikh.*

Book two in the True Love series available now, in audio, paperback and eBook

responsibility for, any author or third-party websites referred to in or on this book.

License Notes

This book is licensed for your personal enjoyment only. This book may not be re-sold or given away to other people. If you would like to share this book with another person, please purchase an additional copy for each recipient.

Published by

Blue Orchid Publishing

New Zealand

Visit www.molliemathews.com to read more about all our books and to buy them. You will also find features, author interviews and news of author events, and you can sign up for e-newsletters so that you're always first to hear about our new releases.

 Created with Vellum

ABOUT THE AUTHOR

MOLLIE MATHEWS writes fun, sophisticated, passion-filled contemporary romance. She is known for her "sensual, beautiful, empowered stories enveloped in true romance" (5-star review). Her books have resonated with a global audience. She has been featured in magazines, television, and radio.

A former child and family therapist Mollie passionately believes in the power of romance to transform people's lives. She loves Mother Theresa's words, *"We are all pens in the hands of a writing God sending love letters to the world."*

Her stories are unashamedly positive, optimistic, full of fun and passion.

She is graduate of Victoria University, in Wellington, New Zealand and has given keynote speeches at romance writers conventions and international seminars.

Mollie follows the sun, dividing her time between New Zealand and exotic locations—wherever she intends setting her next romance novel. She lives with her very own romantic hero, Lorenzo—tall, dark, terribly handsome and fluent in Spanish!

Follow her on BookBub https://www.bookbub.com/authors/mollie-mathews and on her blog https://molliemathews.wordpress.com

and sign up for Mollie's newsletter at www.Molliemathews.com and receive her FREE gift.

Follow Mollie on twitter at www.twitter.com/molliemathewsnz

Join Mollie on Facebook at www.facebook.com/molliemathewsnz

Be inspired by Mollie on Instagram www.instagram.com/molliemathewsauthor

Check out her inspiration board on Pinterest www. nz.pinterest.com/molliemathews/

Writing as Cassandra Gaisford (www.cassandragaisford.com), she is also an award-winning artist and bestselling author of self-empowerment books. Cassandra is celebrated by her readers as, "The Queen of Uplifting Inspiration."

BY MOLLIE MATHEWS

GEMSTONE BILLIONAIRE BRIDES:

THE ITALIAN BILLIONAIRE'S CHRISTMAS BRIDE

THE ITALIAN BILLIONAIRE'S SCANDALOUS MARRIAGE

GEMSTONE BILLIONAIRES 2 BOOK-BUNDLE BOX SET

GEMSTONE BILLIONAIRES 3 BOOK-BUNDLE BOX SET

PASSION DOWN UNDER:

MARRIED BY CHRISTMAS
BRIDE OF GOLD

TRUE LOVE:

FLIGHT of PASSION
CLAIMED by THE SHEIKH

***PASSION DOWN UNDER SASSY
   SHORT STORIES:***

TWIST OF FATE
LOVE ME FOREVER
LOVE ME AS I AM
FOREVER AND ALWAYS
THE LIGHTKEEPER'S LOVER
*PASSION DOWN UNDER 2 BOOK-
   BUNDLE BOX SET (Books 1 & 2)*